FIC
RYA
Ryans, Derek, author.
Take the leap

Take The Leap

SHORT STORIES COLLECTION

Also by Derek Ryans

Short Stories
   Furriest of All
   Losing Control
   Tommy Boy
   No More Misery
   Reunion

Upcoming Novel
   Facing the Mirror, a Novel
   (Work in Progress, Four Chapters Available for Preview)

Available on derekryans.com

Take The Leap

SHORT STORIES COLLECTION

Derek Ryans

DEREK RYANS
2016

PROPERTY OF
SEQUOYAH REGIONAL
LIBRARY SYSTEM

Copyright © 2016 by Derek Ryans

All rights reserved.

This book or any portion thereof may not be reproduced or used in any manner whatsoever without the express written permission of the publisher except for the use of brief quotations in a book review or scholarly journal.

First Printing: 2016

ISBN 978-1-329-80693-1

Derek Ryans
Email: derekryans@notzeroyet.com
www.derekryans.com

DEDICATION

To all those who believed in me and in Not Zero Yet, thank you. You are the reason that I am here today.

To Ms. Wifi, see you soon love.

CONTENTS

Acknowledgements … xi

Preface … xiii

Introduction … xv

58 Days … 1

Shut Up and Kiss Me … 19

Love was in the Lost and Found … 43

ACKNOWLEDGEMENTS

To God – Sometimes I forget to thank you, first and foremost. I'm glad I remembered this time.

To Mom – Through the struggles and tears and more tears, we still managed to put smiles on our faces. Thanks Mom, for giving me space to live inside my imaginary world. For letting me dream even when you were scared that it'd clean out your bank account.

To the girl that I will refer to as "Ms. Wifi" – All my life I tried to match different girls' features to those that I've written in my stories as the must haves for a "perfect girl." It wasn't until I saw you interact with the world and speak whatever's on your mind that I realized I didn't need to try anymore, because the girl that I had written in my stories has literally walked into my life.

To JC – I always thought my first published work would be the book that I showed you. Years have passed and I've gone on to collect memories on my own but I've never stopped thanking you. Thank you for the lessons learned, for the memories shared, and for my wings.

To Kate and Angie – I don't say it enough. You two are absolutely amazing. Thanks for the support and the unwavering confidence. 2016, let's conquer destiny.

To Linda – I still remember when I was in high school, you had said to me, "You really are something, you know that? Your mind...it's out of this world." Thank you for your advice when I launched Not Zero Yet, I hope that this book will honor your memories. RIP.

To the Not Zero Yet Team, photographer Olive Wang, and model Irene – If it wasn't for that Not Zero Yet photo shoot, this book wouldn't exist.

To Kayla Chuang and Michelle Shen – You two were so brave in taking on the challenge of reading this book!

To Kuo Ping Jun – Superman is about to fly!

To Jaylen Empty Baymax BeiQi Kong – Believe in 0.001 right? Thanks for always reminding me.

To Yua Chu and Rebecca – Your hugs and encouragement saved me.

To SY Tan – It never ceases to amaze me how hard you work for someone that you don't even like. Thank you for stepping out of your comfort zone.

To Damien Peng and Melissa Lee – When I needed friends that didn't make me speak Chinese, God dropped guardian angels in my lap.

To my friends and family all over the world – I wouldn't be here today without you all. Thank you. I love you.

PREFACE

I really wish I had something smart to say here. That I always believed in destiny and I wanted to write a love story about two people who were meant to be. But the truth is...it all started with a themed photo shoot for my t-shirt line, Not Zero Yet. One of the design series was called NZY Zodiacs – I took the Chinese zodiac signs and I turned them into designs for my shirts. When it came time to do a photo shoot, I thought it would be cool to do a "destiny theme." And so I came up with the idea of a street musician wanting to save a homeless guy.

That's what started it all. And it was supposed to be just one story.

After I had written *58 Days*, the feedback that I got was that I left the story unfinished. To be perfectly honest, I really enjoyed writing *58 Days* and I myself was curious what would happen with Ethan and Charity, so I continued on to write Shut Up and Kiss Me.

When I wrote *Shut Up and Kiss Me*, I was a bit uncomfortable because I was afraid that I couldn't get into the mindset of a girl. It turned out to be so much fun and great research for my other work in progress, *Facing the Mirror*.

I thought two stories would've ended it but the feedback I got was surprising, to say the least. *Love Was in the Lost and Found* was the longest of the three stories because people were genuinely showing interest in the story between Ethan and Charity. The readers had responded that I left them hanging twice and they want an ending.

So there it is, I wrote three stories for fun and never thought about publishing them. And now they are a collection of stories for people to read and enjoy. Never say never, because the limits you set in your mind are challenges for life to break. As a lot of us know by now, there's no winning when you go against life.

I sincerely hope you enjoy reading these stories.

Derek Ryans

INTRODUCTION

Take the Leap Short Stories Collection includes three short stories:

- 58 Days
- Shut Up and Kiss Me
- Love was in the Lost and Found

58 DAYS

If a person asked me what the sky looks like right now, I'd answer, "It looks like a child decided to play paintball with God and He lost on purpose." Blue and orange colors blot the canvas that we mere human beings look upon. But no one is going to talk to me. Fifty-seven days ago, people who ran into me would at least gesture a hello or stop for a small talk. Now? They barely even look at me. And when they do, it's to let me know that they want me to keep a safe distance. There is a sweet smell in the air, which could be a good and a bad thing. If it rains, the hot air that emanates from the concrete will be bearable, and I will have some kind of a shower. On the other hand, I'll look and smell like a wet dog.

Oh, there go those shoes again, the hole in the left shoe gets bigger each time I see them. Right when the sun is about to come up and morning joggers are heading to the beach, those shoes approach. Their owner keeps a safe distance as well. It intrigues me though. Why doesn't she just take them off? Maybe her toes like breathing fresh air.

What really fascinates me, is how she sets up the sign. The very first day she showed up with the sign, it was blown away into the street. It didn't stand very well to begin with, and after it had a little run-in with a pickup, it didn't stand at all. So what did she do? She laid it on the ground and used her guitar case to hold it down. Silly right? Well, today she's back with a new sign. After last night's rain, even the sign gave in. That rain showed her no mercy. But she's back again, with a new and actual-standing sign that inherited the same ideals as the last one:

Love, Music, Save the World

Ha.

And the guitar tuning starts. Girlie girl, that's not how a guitar is tuned! Hell, a beer donation will get her a well-tuned guitar. Fifty-seven days now, doesn't she have better things to do? Some place to be? Maybe she got into a fight with daddy...but look at those hands...the calluses...no... she's not a daddy's little girl.

And that hair, the way it glows in the sun. Till the rain comes down, of course, then the hair does something wonderful. It becomes the color of her alluring brown eyes. The two complement each other so well that I could almost put down my drink.

Almost.

The good news is I still have some rum left; now where did I leave that bottle? I reach into the box that I carried out of what used to be my house. These empty bottles can be traded for a bit of cash; I have no clue where but I know it's possible. Instead of chasing me off, the building manager gave me a tip about my bottles. I don't think she realized some of them weren't empty. Finally, I pick up a bottle that weighs just a tad heavier than the others. Come here my sweet. You can tell it's good rum when it gets better over time. This is definitely not one of them. Tastes like piss. Still, it's a drink. Thanks to the old man for his liquor donations when he gave me the boot huh?

"You chose the bottles over your family," Dad had told me. "You can have the bottles."

No old man, I chose the bottles over you. Hit my mom

again and I'll be smashing your face with one of these. But she didn't exactly try to keep me.

Tears, oh the tears.

"Please, Tom! Give me a chance to be a better wife for you," Mom had cried and held on to Dad's leg as she crawled. "I know I can!"

So I left. Me and my bottles. And here I am.

Who's the girl? There's not one clue in my mind as to who she is. She walked out of her building one day, exactly fifty-seven days ago, paused as if she saw a ghost and then she turned and went back inside. When she came out again, she had a guitar and a cardboard sign. Whether the scorching sun and the killer humidity are doing their dance or the playful rain decides to cut in, she's here. I'm almost certain her skin is weather proof. Her hair, however, not so much, she does everything she can to protect her hair. What I would do to mess up that always-perfectly-combed hair. I imagine it would be quite soft, slipping right through my fingers. These are just dreams of course. My dirt-covered fingers are only fit for grasping bottles now. The calluses on the tips of my fingers are always just a shade darker.

I remember grabbing my wallet that night, I cleared out the liquor cabinet, but my sweet Misery, oh the old bastard had put her away somewhere I couldn't reach. The songs that I had written with Misery were the songs that got me through the darkest nights. She and I shared drinks over string changes. We shed tears through tunings.

"Ethan, please!" Mom pleaded. "Just apologize to your father!"

That sting on my cheek, Dad's ring imprinting into my jaw, I will not cry, I will not back down, I will protect my mother. I swing and hit nothing. Something tastes salty in my mouth. I swing and swing and swing. It suddenly occurred to me that this man never taught me how to fight. As many times as he had raised his fist, never once did he teach me self-defense. I guess it makes sense, would you train your son to fight if you were beating him?

I heard his voice. I saw Misery in his hand.

"No, Dad...please!" It had been the first time I called him dad in years.

"You love this guitar so much it should become part of you," Dad raised Misery in the air with both hands.

"Please! Dad!"

At first, it was a little bit of a sting. Then the room spun, a little. And a little bit of blood on my fingers. And a little bit of Misery embedded into my skull.

"Oh, Tom," Mom cried. "Your shoulders! You shouldn't lift anything that high!"

Mom and Dad started to disappear. When I came to, it was just like always, me and sweet Misery in my room. Except something was a little different this time. Misery was much smaller than when I first got her. I grasped her strings in my hand. The strings that once made me bleed. I collected pieces of her, and I sat planning her revenge.

Revenge I wanted and seven days were all I had. My friend was kind enough to give me seven days. He knew that my dad would somehow find me there, and there'd be hell to pay. No one goes against the great Tom Winston. Seven must have been my lucky number because the amount of money I had in my bank was seven hundred seventy dollars. I tried calling different schools, restaurants, even the local 7-Eleven, no one would even give me an application. On the seventh day that I was out of the house, my cell phone had stopped working. My friend informed me that my dad had told him I should either go home or hit the streets. In a small developing town where everyone knew my dad, my only weapon against him would be if I found a way out. So I went to the bank to take all my money out, but dear old Dad thought of that too. When I walked out into the parking lot, my car had disappeared! The people who took my car were quite humorous, they left me my duffle bag and a box of liquor bottles.

    I carried my box of bottles to a nearby building, hoping to at least recycle them before I figured out my new game plan. The old lady who managed the building told me to hold on to the bottles and she'd help me get some money for them. I had taken a seat against the wall in the corner, and I must have fallen asleep because when I woke up again, I was covered in a blanket. There was a note on my duffel bag, "This blanket belonged to my granddaughter, why don't you rest here till you're ready to go home?"

    I slept outside the building for a night, and I left the box outside the trash room. I knew the owner of a restaurant and thought maybe I could've traded my phone for some food and enough cash to get a bus ticket. He took my phone and offered to let me sleep in the storage room behind the restaurant. I had food and a place to stay for a whole two days before his son came and beat the living crap out of me. The moment that my face hit the cold concrete I knew that my only chance of survival would be that apartment building.

The rest...well, I'm sure you know how the story goes.

"Thank you!" I hear the girl's voice.

I turn to see a couple standing by the girl. They throw some change into her guitar case. Maybe a dollar, maybe less, and the girl thanks them. She strums her guitar, singing songs I'd never heard of, but I really must admit the songs are quite good. I sip my rum and allow myself to drift into a peaceful bliss. Yes, I said peaceful bliss. Did you want me to sip rum and cry?

"I wish you could know me the way I know you," she sings. "Let me save you...hold you..."

The song comes to an end. My bottle is officially empty. Damn.

"Hey, girlie girl!" I call out. She cocks her head sideways and looks at me.

"Yes, I'm talking to you," I say.

"My name is not girlie girl," she says.

"It is to me," I reply.

At that moment, it was as if a sheet of ice draped over the air between us.

"Kidding. Kidding. Sorry, what's your name?"

"Charity," she walks over to me and extends her hand.

The calluses on her hand reveal that she plays guitar, but she's not a guitar player. And her hand is clean, cleaner than mine at least. I press my palm into the ground.

"You're kidding me, right? 'Love, music, save the world' and your name is Charity," I say.

She bites her bottom lip and steps back.

"I wasn't trying to be mean..." I stare down at my permanently stained shirt. "Sorry, I'm not good with people."

"I know who you are," she says. "Tom Winston's son."

"I am," I say. "And who's your dad?"

"You can go home, you know?" she says. "Everyone knows where you are and what you do; your dad just won't let them bother you."

My hand separates itself from the ground and clutches onto the wooden piece hanging on my necklace, my Misery.

"People take photos of you and post them on Facebook," Charity walks back towards her sign and sits down on the sidewalk. "You're not as invisible as you want to be, or you make yourself out to be."

"Should I smile for your camera then?" I ask.

"Do you see a camera on me?"

I grin. And right then and there, I could swear I saw it, a genuine smile on her face. The corners of her lips curled up.

"How much do you get, standing here all day?" I ask.

"Sometimes twenty bucks, sometimes nothing," she strums her guitar. "It depends. You should know. You're like twenty feet away from me."

"You're assuming I actually look at you," I rearrange the bottles in the box, wondering if maybe she'd buy me a drink.

"Maybe I'm here because standing by you will get me exposure, and I'll be a YouTube sensation." She stands up and turns her back towards me.

"That's an idea. Music, love, save the world, stand next to the homeless Ethan Winston and you're an instant celebrity."

She carefully sets her guitar down and walks away. Where's she going? I wanted to ask her to buy me a drink! She's not leaving her guitar...is she? She disappears around the corner. I walk over to her guitar and pick it up. It's no Misery, but it's not bad. Should I take it and run? And if I ran...will I ever see those brown eyes again?

I strum a chord. Eeesh, wrong chord. Try a different one, ahh yes, that's it.

"I wish you could know me the way I know you," I sing. "Let me save you...hold you..." I don't really remember the rest of the song, but I remember the melody. So I'm humming. And humming.

"If I could hold you tight, I'd show you how brightly you shine," Charity's voice joins my humming.

My fingers stop mid strum. I look at my feet. My dirty feet. I had gotten into a fight with someone and needless to say, I lost. Their trophy: my shoes. I miss my shoes. I miss Misery.

Charity hands me a bottle of water. I can't even look at her. I set her guitar against the wall and walk back to my corner. She follows me and sets the water bottle down as I slip against the wall. I want to look at her and thank her, but I find myself staring at the shorts that I have been wearing for almost two months. I bet she can smell the stench on me. I know I can. She takes a pair of flip flops out of the plastic bag in her hand and sets them down.

"They should fit," she says and walks back over to her side.

"Can I—" I start to say.

"Hmmm?" She turns to look at me and her eyes pierce through mine. I wish I could tell her to stop doing that. Those eyes...I see them even after she leaves every day.

"Can I maybe borrow a few bucks," I ask. "Just enough for a beer."

She doesn't answer me. She strums her guitar and hums. I take the flip flops and set them beside the box. I will wear them when my feet are clean. I lift the box by its sides and there's a rip. Bottles fall through and crash like dominoes. I dive into the pile with my hands aimed at the flip flops. She looks over at me. One flip flop in my hand, the other on the ground. She rolls her eyes. Well...that was unnecessary wasn't it? I was trying to save them for when I can clean my feet! What's the use of me explaining anything?

I pick up the bottle of water and open it, tapping my feet a bit to get a sense of a melody. "You want to save me?" I start to sing while I pour the water onto the ground. "Too late."

She looks at me wide-eyed and nostrils flared. I think I see a tear. I want to stop singing. I want to wipe those tears from her eyes. I'm sorry girlie girl...I'm so sorry. This is for the best.

"In a world so cold, I'm used to being alone. Please, don't come close..." I can't look at her. I can't...breathe.

The sound of the zipping guitar case travels through the space between us as my eyes fixate on my dirt-colored feet.

Maybe I should've used that water to wash them. Would that make her a little less mad? Diminishing footstep sounds follow. A final sound of a thump and she vanishes. She left her sign. It lays flat on the ground. A few hours go by, or at least I think a few hours had gone by. I lost my watch too, in another fight; not a homeless guy.

The sign, "Love, Music, Save the World," really just a piece of a cardboard cutout, lies in wait for its owner to return. Some people walk by as if there isn't a decent sized piece of cardboard in front of them and others were kind enough to walk around it. Children make it a game to see if they can hop over it, most of them can't. And another type of douchebag, they are too busy on their cell phones to realize they walked over it.

I look around. She's seriously not coming back this time. Before more kids can come and practice their long jump skills, I swoop in and set the sign up against the wall. No one will take it, right? Should be okay...

I walk off to the back of the building where the apartment manager's office is. Some boxes are sitting outside, so I helped myself to one and brought it to back to my spot. The bottles fit quite well! I need something to be proud of every once in a while.

"Excuse me?" The voice sounds young. I look up to see a little girl, couldn't have been more than twelve years old. "Where's the girl that sings? My mom said I could come for five minutes today."

"Uhhh...you know what, sweetheart? I think she felt sick today and had to go home."

"But her sign is here," the little girl points. "And somebody made it dirty."

"Yeah...ummm...I'll clean it up for her." The girl walks away without even hearing my answer. Thanks. Really. I'm invisible huh? Stupid sign...

I move the box of bottles to the back of the building and knock on the office door. No answer. What do I do now? A drink right now would be nice, it's not a necessity of course, but it would just be nice. They say drinking clouds your judgment and I need that. The more I drink, the less likely I am to crawl back to my dad. I also have an urge to see Charity. Ha. Charity...the girlie girl who wants to save the world.

"Found a different place to stay?" The apartment manager comes up behind me.

"No...just...I think I'm going to get rid of these bottles," I say. "I doubt I can get much for them."

The old woman searches in her purse and pulls out a set of keys. She moves her glasses to the top of her head and examines the keys. I look down at my clothes that have been smudged with everything on God's great earth. If I'm going to talk to Charity, I should probably find a way to get cleaned up.

"You know Ethan...some day you have to fight your battles," the old woman walks over to the side door next to the office. I follow her. Once inside the trash collection room, I pick out a few bottles and set them to the side. The rest go into the recycling bin. There's a large broken box in the corner and I ask if I could have it. She nods.

"Need something to sleep on? I could see if I have another blanket in the office."

"No, no thank you. I'm…going to make something."

"Oh?"

"I'll show you when I'm done, okay? You'll be in the office right?"

"Yes. Yes, that's where I will be," she says and walks towards the door, but then she stops. "Ethan?"

"Yes, ma'am?"

"Charity is a sweet girl," the woman says. "She lives alone, in 12B. Nobody asks you to leave because once a week she cooks for all the tenants in the building."

"What's she doing playing music for money?" I ask.

"Son, isn't that something you should find out?" The old woman walks out and closes the door behind her.

Apartment 12B, I can go and apologize. But look at me. What am I going to say? I've been watching you for fifty-seven days and I think I'm in love with you? There is no future with me. I don't even know where I'll be tomorrow. Just leave it. But I don't want to leave it. I want…I want…her…

I pull the large broken box from the corner and kick it. With a skip and a hop, I get on top of it and rip its sides off. I'm screaming, but I can't hear my voice. All I can hear is Charity's song. "If I could hold you tight…I'd show you how brightly you shine…" Tears flow freely and race down my cheeks. Am I even a man? Couldn't stand up to my father. Couldn't win fights in the street. In here, bawling like a little boy. When will I ever stand on my own?

The door creaks open; someone comes in with a pile of

boxes in his hands. He glances at me, sets the boxes down and rushes back out the door. He must be doing some house cleaning. One box had an old mop, computer cables, glue, all sorts of weird stuff you really don't think you'd ever need in your life. An idea comes to my mind. I rummage through other recycled things. No, it's not like the movies where you find treasure in trash. You just find—trash and a broken fishing rod.

    I must have spent a couple of hours in the garbage room because when I open the door again, a tinted marble blue sky and a slight breeze welcome me into the night. With my back against the wall, I edge stealthily to the front of the building and peek around the corner. Charity's sign is still there, just the sign. I lay down a few feet away from it and hum that song. That stupid song Charity sings.

    When I close my eyes I see her so clearly. The straight brown hair that never looks out of place. The big smile that she has on her face. The way she covers her mouth when she laughs. The look in her eyes like she's hiding something. Girlie girl...what do you have to hide? She smiles when she sings but even then...there's a hint of sadness in her voice. I'm not fascinated by her. I'm just a little curious. Just a little...

    A faint guitar sound wakes me. It's either she was in my dreams last night and I heard her guitar strums or Charity's back. The sky is blue and orange again. She's plucking random strings but her sign is not up. I push myself off the ground and walk over to where I left the sign. The guitar strumming stops. She's leaning against her guitar and staring off into the air. I put the sign down in front of her and set it up. She kicks it over.

"I know it's a stupid sign, alright?" she heaves a sigh.

I'm trying to find the words to say but nothing comes out. Something catches my eyes behind the wall and I walk back over to my side. The old lady leaves some food or drinks for me from time to time. I found a bottle of water and a sandwich along with a note, "You can't run from your battles forever."

I walk over to Charity and offer her the bottle of water. "I'm sorry…"

She stands and faces me. Her eyes, it's as if they're empty. I want to pull her close and wrap my arms around her. Instead, I find myself just standing there, unable to move my eyes away from her. She takes the water bottle from me and opens the cap. From the corner of my eyes, I see her lifting an arm in the air and water begins to trickle down my forehead. I can't be sure if it's the water in my eyes or she's got tears in her eyes too. The water makes its way down my neck, into my shirt, all the way down to my toes.

"I found you…" I say. "Or maybe you found me…I don't know."

She blinks and a tear rolls down her cheek. I wipe my hand on my wet shirt. Is it clean? Clean enough, I suppose. I reach out and wipe her tear with the tip of my thumb.

"I'm sorry…" I say. "I'm never going to be good enough for you, but dammit, every time you come close to me I feel alive! It's the lamest thing I've ever said but it's true."

The empty water bottle hits the ground with a thud. She looks at me blankly. I take her hand and place it on my cheek.

"Today's the fifty-eighth day I've been watching you, I think... No. I know. I'm in love with you."

She looks at me, her eyes growing wider and wider, her hand raises in the air. My cheekbone felt it first, the touch of the ring she's wearing. And a sting. A sting that lasts longer than my dad's punches. She spins on her heels and runs off. The wet concrete slips under my knees as I kneel to the ground.

Apparently when you say that you love someone, it's something you don't plan...and the reaction is also something you don't plan. And the moment that you realized it's too late, it really is too late. It's a good thing I guess, that she ran. I'm not good for her. So...everything's good, I'll just...go back to my drinks that I have no money for. I'll just... walk back over to my corner. And I do. I sit. And do nothing. Because that's just who I am. I do...nothing.

Sitting out in the sun just about baked my clothes dry. And I must have dozed off because when I open my eyes again, I could swear I see her sitting not too far from me. The fallen sign is still between us. Am I delusional? If she is real, and the sun is not tricking me, what is she doing here? What do I say to her?

The scorching concrete press into my feet as I stand and run to the back of the building. I knock frantically and someone else answers the door.

"Can I help you?" he asks.

"Uh...the old lady...she's not here?" I ask.

"She's doing her rounds," the man says. "You've caused her enough trouble already."

"I apologize," I say. "But please, this is important. Can you please open the side door for me? The trash room."

"I cannot let you go sifting through trash son."

"Please sir...I left something there. Something important."

"Whatever you left there, isn't yours! It belongs to our tenants, even if it's trash, it's their trash."

"Let me get this one thing and I will leave this building."

The man looks at me and folds his arms. "You will leave?"

"Yes."

"Today?"

"Right now."

He takes his keys out of his pocket and walks over to the side door. He opens it and nods for me to go in. I look behind the trash bins and pick up the cardboard leaning against the wall.

"Thank you, you won't see me in front of the building anymore, that's a promise."

Once I got back to the front of the building, I set the cardboard down next to Charity. Her head lifts from the guitar she's leaning on and looks at my recycled creation.

There are seven liquor bottles on the board, tied with fishing lines to spell out the letters L, V and E. The letter O was made from glued together beer bottle caps. She gasps and covers her mouth.

"Thank you for saving me from myself," I say. "I guess this is goodbye..." I stand over her and smooth out her hair. She

58 *Days* 16

flinches. "Sorry, always wanted to do that."

I must be high on something stupid because I lean in and kiss her forehead. She doesn't move at all. Or maybe she can't.

"Bye..." I turn to leave.

She grabs my wrist and says, "I have a couch..."

SHUT UP AND KISS ME

He fits on my couch perfectly, curled up with his head buried under pillows, clutching the blanket covering him. Like a big lap dog...I've always wanted to adopt a big dog. Did I just compare a human being to a dog? I feel a little guilty I suppose, but really, if you could see him lying there on the couch, like a big puppy!

Let me tell you something about this guy—he's no ordinary human being. I've known him my entire life and he still doesn't recognize me. I used to visit during the summers when I was little but when I moved to town, girls from my department talked about him like he was some kind of a god. His dad is the dean of the local music school; I moved here for that school. That, and my grandma took me in when my parents died.

I can't believe it's been four years already. The stories I've heard about Ethan Winston over the last four years make me wonder why I spent the last two months sitting next to him outside my building. It makes me wonder why I let him stay on my couch last night. Ethan Winston, the guy who has been known to sleep with anything that walks, leaves trails of broken hearts behind everywhere he goes and still manages to make girls think he's a good man. Did I let the wolf into my house? And if I did, I did so willingly. What does that say about me? He bought other girls gifts, drinks, and dinners before taking them to bed. I took him off the streets, gave him a couch, and no sex.

You must be wondering—do I want to have sex with him? No. Absolutely not. But after hearing stories for so long, it was hard to resist...I just wanted to see if he truly is that much of a scumbag. Ethan Winston the wonder boy has fallen, and one day, fifty-nine days ago, he fell on my doorstep. And yesterday, the fifty-eighth day, he told me he was in love with me. Who does he think he is? I'm saving myself for someone special, not him. He's probably got more STDs than Paris Hilton.

"Girlie girl..." he says.

I look over at him, messy bed hair, stretching his arm and scratching his chest. What exactly do girls see in him? I don't see it.

"What are you doing sitting on the floor?" he asks.

"The couch was full," I say. It's not. But I want to pretend it is. If I sit closer to him, I might do something stupid.

I might strangle him.

He springs up quickly, slipping his feet into the flip flops I bought him. He says, "I'm sorry, here's your couch back."

"Maybe I like the floor," I say. "The clothes look like a perfect fit."

I find myself ripping tiny little pieces of carpet with my fingers.

He's just standing there. I think my joke about the couch really scared him. Nothing about him fits the stories people have told me. Yesterday when I opened the door and walked into my house, he stayed outside like a vampire that has to be invited in or something. He stood at my door, one hand holding his flip flops, the other holding my cardboard sign and my guitar across his shoulders. What was I carrying? Nothing. He probably does it for all the girls. But the next

Shut Up and Kiss Me 20

thing that happened, it was...cute...

I told him to come in, that he could get cleaned up and eat something. He stood outside but stretched himself in, setting my guitar and sign down by the wall. He held onto his flip flops. And he just stood there.

"Last time I checked, flip flops are for your feet..." I said, a little annoyed that he just won't put them on. They're not the best kind, I know, I couldn't afford the hundred-dollar flip flops that his dad used to buy him.

"My feet are dirty..." he said, looking down at his feet. "I don't want to ruin the flip flops...and I don't want to mess up your floor."

You know that look a puppy has when it pees on the floor and knows it's done something wrong? That look was written all over Ethan's face. If he was acting, someone please give him an Oscar and get him out of my life, because I bought every bit of it. I got him a wet towel and watched him sit outside my door cleaning his feet. I thought I even saw tears in his eyes.

Suddenly I notice hand in front of me, moving in a steady up and down motion, bringing me back to the present.

"Are you ok?" Ethan asks.

I pinch myself. Do not blush, Charity, DO NOT BLUSH.

"Yeah, just thinking about something," I say.

"I should probably get going..." he says. "Can you tell your brother I'm sorry? I don't know when I'd be able to wash these clothes and return them to him."

Shut Up and Kiss Me

I don't have a brother. I bought those clothes for Ethan last month, took them home and then took the elevator twelve floors down to realize I had no idea how to hand the clothes to him. Finally, yesterday, when I told him he could take a shower, I handed him the clothes and said they were my brother's clothes.

"Where are you going?" I ask. "Home?"

His head drops again. He does that every time I ask him about home. He touches his necklace. Actually, I wouldn't say it's a necklace, it's more of a string—a piece of string with what looks like a piece of wood hanging from it.

"Thanks for letting me crash here last night," he says. "I'll find someplace else to stay."

I want to hit him. *Screw it. I'm going to do it.* He's standing close enough to me so I hit his calf. I know. What the hell? I hit his calf!

He jumps.

"Sit," I say. And he sits. Seriously, I know I keep comparing him to a dog, but now you see what I mean, right? Maybe this is his appeal to all the girls. But not me, of course. If I wanted a dog, I'd get one.

"Stay here till you figure something out. I'm tired of seeing people post 'Ethan sightings' on Facebook. It's like a new game or something. No one ever offered a place for you to stay?"

"I traded my phone for food because I was hungry," he taps his fingers on the floor, completely in sync with my carpet-ripping rhythm. I hate him. I hate him so much. "Haven't been on Facebook since...I don't remember when."

Silly me, I forgot who his father is. If grandma was here right now she'd probably "strongly advise" me to stay away from Tom Winston's son.

"Tom Winston is the devil in human form," grandma used to say. "People say his wife always wears heavy makeup to hide the bruises. My Charity, remember to be more like your mother. That woman never wore makeup. Don't you hide your scars, girl."

I miss you, Grandma. If only you can be here to stop me from what I'm doing now. I let the devil's son into my house, maybe even my heart. He counted the days that he watched me. I used to watch him every summer. Then I moved here, and there were all these stories about him. I was afraid of him for years. In one day's time, he knocked down every single defense I had ever built against him, just in case he and I ever met.

And the worst thing is, I'm the one who went looking for him. He looked hurt, sleeping on the sidewalk outside. I posted a note in the lobby about free lunch once a week and asked the old lady downstairs not to chase him away. I don't know how the son of the great Tom Winston could end up on the street but he did. And as many stories as I've heard about him taking girls to bed, none of those beds gave him a place to stay. The girls that said they'd gladly sleep with him. The girls that said they were "madly in love" with Ethan, the musical prodigy. No one offered him a place of security. Forgive me, Grandma, I brought him into the apartment that you left me, and no, he hasn't touched me; don't worry.

Is that bacon I smell?

I turn to look at the kitchen and there's Ethan, cooking.

Shut Up and Kiss Me

He really took it seriously when I told him to make himself at home. He has taken all the trash out, including some heavy things I've been meaning to throwing out. Ethan said he wanted to earn his keep. And now he's cooking. Does he do this for every girl? I don't want to become one of his girls. What am I talking about? I don't want to be his girl, period. End of story.

"You look like a sunny-side-up kinda girl," Ethan says, turning to look at me, brown bangs nearly covering his eyes, and a towel hanging over his shoulder. I've always thought that he was a bit on the chubby side, that he hadn't lost his baby fat. Now the sunlight shines on him through the kitchen window, I see what other girls see when they look at him the morning after: boyish charm with broad shoulders. So that's his appeal. Good. I don't do boyish charm and I like my men skinny. So I'm good.

"I actually don't like to eat breakfast."

That is a big fat lie. I love sunny-side-up eggs. I just don't want him to know he's right. Ethan smirks when he knows he's right and he's doing it now. It makes me want to grab him and kiss him. Wait, what? I didn't say kiss him. I said kill him.

He puts the plates on the table and motions for me to join him. I try to appear reluctant as I get up.

Okay, okay, I admit it, alright? I like the fact that he didn't get anywhere close to my bed last night and he's making me breakfast today. If he does this for all the girls he sleeps with, well then I'm a big doofus. But even a doofus has to eat. He hands me a glass of juice as I grab a seat at the dining table. He sets a paper towel, a fork and knife in front of me. Is it just me or he never looks at me? I thought he said he was "in love with me." Well, lover boy, why won't you look at me?

"Eat up, girlie girl," he cuts his bacon into even pieces. "Gonna need energy if you want to save the world.

The bacon looks crisp, delicious. The eggs are perfectly done, looking delicious. Even the glass of juice is filled just right, so picture perfect. I despise picture perfect. I push the food around a little bit with my fork. I take a quick bite and... well, you know, it's bacon and eggs. He makes them the way grandma did. I hate him. He's so focused on eating his food I'll just let him eat. I don't like it when the yolk reaches the edge of the plate, so I scrape up the yellow goo and wipe it on the toast. Maybe I can make a smiley face or something.

"You want me to cook something else so your smiley face can have hair, ears, things like that?" Ethan looks at me with his head tilted to the side. I look at him. He immediately looks at his food.

"If you're gonna stay here," I say as I push all the bacon to the side (I like to hear them crunch, one at a time), "we need some ground rules."

"Yes, ma'am," he says, looking up at me quickly, and then back to his food. I can tell he's hungry. I think he wants to pick up his plate and lick it.

"Don't call me ma'am," I take a sip of juice and stare at him.

"Yes, girlie girl," he wipes his mouth with a paper towel and folds it neatly, like his dirty clothes that he folded and then put on top of a plastic bag on my floor. He takes his plate and stands up.

Shut Up and Kiss Me

"Don't call me 'girlie girl' either. I have a name. Show some respect."

"You always this serious, Charity?" he asks, standing no more than a foot away from me, holding his empty plate in his hand. He takes a piece of bacon off of my plate and feeds it to me. His eyes looking directly into mine, those dark brown pupils that are always avoiding me are now making my toes wiggle. I taste bacon but I swear I did not willingly open my mouth. I hear the crunch of bacon. I see his eyes. His questioning eyes. His eyes that seem to be trying to penetrate my mind. Not today, Ethan Winston. Not today. I push him away.

"No petting my head, no feeding me!" I scream.

"Noted," he says, already by the kitchen sink. Is it just me or does he know my house a little too well?

Look at the rest of the bacon on the plate, they're all jealous of the one I just ate. The one Ethan fed me. The one I unwillingly ate. He's doing the dishes, mumbling about how I should hurry up and finish my bacon so that he can finish doing the dishes. I wonder if I wait a little longer, would he dare to try to feed me again? If he does, I'll kick him where it hurts. Even his children that he creates from this day on will remember me.

And just like that, the days of my singing on the street corner end. It's time for me to go back to my real job. My grandma passed away and left me her music shop. I went from being the piano teacher to the owner in the split-second that my grandma dropped to the floor from a heart attack.

"Stay strong, darling" were the last words she said to me in the ambulance. By the time we reached the hospital, she was dead.

When I took over the store, my grandma's friend, Charlie, helped me ease into the situation. I'm pretty sure he and Grandma had a fling. Neither of them would admit it, but it was in their eyes. As Grandma always said, the eyes never lie. So when I told Charlie I wanted to play guitar in the front of my building for a while, maybe it will attract some clients into our store, he gladly said he'd watch the store for me. But his eyes said something different. When he closed the store on the very first day and came to "surprise" me, he saw Ethan.

Unlike Grandma, Charlie is very fond of Ethan. He treated Ethan like his own son. I'm not sure if it's just a rumor...but I've heard stories about Ethan's dad forbidding him to come to my store. I think it was my sophomore year in college when I saw him in my store every week for a few months. He seemed to be waiting for somebody, but that person never showed. So Charlie kept him company.

Whenever Ethan came to the store, Veronica, our part-time helper/my classmate would give my grandma the heads up and she would send me to the back. Grandma would always find something for me to do, and it would never be anything in the front of the store. I'd lurk around in the hallway and peek. The store's not that big and I could see pretty easily everything that goes on. Veronica would always look at Ethan with dreamy eyes. Ethan would smile back, and you can tell he liked her a little. I remember telling Veronica not to sleep with him, she would probably regret it. Then she graduated, met a guy, and they moved away. I never heard from her again.

You know what's great about me talking to you? I'm

Shut Up and Kiss Me

already locked in my room and getting dressed. In high school, a friend of mine told me that if I wore black underwear, then it means I'd have sex that night. So last night after I showered, I put on some really ugly cream colored granny panties. I'm skinny, very skinny, so the granny panties are a little loose. I probably shouldn't wear a dress today. But it's my first day back to the store and I'm bringing Ethan. I want to look nice. Mainly because I own the store of course. Jeans and a t-shirt seem too "girlie girl." I don't want to be his girlie girl. But it is hot outside...maybe I'll wear shorts. My jean shorts. I like them. They're cut off and I think they're sexy but my friends say they're borderline slutty. Every good girl has a bit of a wild side, no? A good girl with granny panties and short shorts, oh yeah, that will definitely keep Ethan away. I pull on a t-shirt and look into the mirror. Suddenly I see a flashback from the previous day.

"I'm in love with you..." he had said. And yet today he says nothing. Pretends like nothing happened. Does he really expect me to just forget something like that? I woke up this morning remembering the feel of his lips on my forehead. He could've kissed me. I would've slapped him or punched him, but he could've kissed me. And he kissed my forehead. How many foreheads have those lips landed on before me?

Snap out of it, Charity. You're trying to help him get back on his feet. That's all. You hate him. All the stories about him are true. Now brush your hair, open your door, and go.

I open my door and he had just come out of the bathroom. He has a bag of trash in his hand. There's another bag of trash in the kitchen. He really takes earning his keep to a whole new level. I'm not a pig but...my house is clean when I have friends over and that's it.

"Come with me to the store today, ok? I think I can find something for you to do."

"Store?" he asks.

"Yeah, Musical Healings, I own it. Well, my grandma did. Now I do."

"Matilda Nash is your grandmother? Oh wow...she was my piano teacher when I was little..." Ethan says. "I see where you get your kindness from."

"Another rule: Do not talk about my grandmother."

"Sorry...can I just say one thing?"

I sigh. This boy. Guy. Man. He just always has to push my limits doesn't he?

"One thing," I say.

"One time I had a cold and messed up at the piano recital," Ethan sits on the couch and for some reason, my feet just carry me towards him. "My dad locked me in a room away from the other contestants. He tied my hands with a belt, saying that I need my fingers for playing. And he kicked me. He kicked me so hard that I spit out blood. When he was done, he opened the door, and there was Ms. Matilda. She slapped my dad with such force that I nearly jumped for joy. I never got to learn piano from your grandma again. And, I never got to thank her. I think she avoided me when I went to the store. But God bless her soul...she was a good woman."

I swear if every word that comes out of Ethan's mouth is a scheme to sleep with me, I will kill him. I want to cry. But I can't. Not in front of him. I wonder if my face looks like I have "kiss me" written all over it, because that's how I feel. I'll

Shut Up and Kiss Me

admit it this one time, only this time. Right now, I wish he'd just kiss me. Every good girl should make a mistake once or twice.

But he doesn't kiss me. He stands up, claps his hands like a little child, excited that we're going to the music store. He had this one chance and he blew it. Ugh! I want to hit him. I want to hit him hard. Why are men so stupid?

The car ride to the store is another thing that amuses me about Ethan. He knows every single song on the radio. No kidding! The dude's been sleeping on a sidewalk for two months and yet he can hum every single song on the radio. My car's my sing-along heaven but I keep silent. I want to see if there was even one song he couldn't hum to. He hummed all the way to the store. Didn't ask about me, didn't ask about the store; I think as long as there's music, his mind just drifts away.

It's a good thing, because I don't want to talk to him. I don't have answers for anything. I just want to listen to his humming. It's a soothing sound. He taps his right foot to the music and you can tell he's trying really hard to keep his hands from moving, but they just move to the music. No, it's not cute, and I'm not watching him. I just keep running into really long lights today.

The bell chimes when the store door opens; I have missed that sound. This place is my home away from home. Charlie comes with an open embrace that takes me by surprise. Really, he's not the hugging type.

"My boy!" Charlie yells and walks past me and right to Ethan. "Have you forgotten this old man?"

Surprise...surprise...the hug is for the wonder boy. Did I

mention I hate him? I hate him so much.

"Charity...uhhh...dug me out of trash," Ethan says.

Charlie looks at me with his all-knowing eyes. "Did she now?"

Ethan scratches his head a bit and explains that an unsuccessful move out of his dad's house landed him on the street for a few months.

"And you didn't come talk to me?" Charlie asks. "I have a ranch not too far from here. Plenty of rooms!"

By "not too far from here" what he means is a thirty-minute drive every day. That's an hour to and from. I look over at Ethan and I see that he has tears rolling down his cheeks. Charlie hugs him and rubs his shoulders, the two of them walk out of the store and disappear into the parking lot.

I walk over to the guitar section and pick out a nice looking one. I own the store; it doesn't mean I know the guitars. Charlie's still working on teaching me that. I remember when Charlie saw Ethan sitting in front of my building.

Charlie called me that night and said, "Save my boy, Charity. Please. Save my boy. I can offer him a place to stay, but I think you want to offer him a home." And he hung up. I didn't call him back. He's never mentioned it again.

All the times that I've watched Ethan, I've never seen him as close to anyone as he is to Charlie. I always thought that he didn't spend time with his dad because he was busy surrounding himself with girls. Even when he came to the store, he and Veronica smiled at each other so much, it made me want to tell them to get a room already. Right before we all graduated, Ethan came to the store and handed Veronica a little box. Two days later she was wearing a new necklace around her neck.

I'm not going to think about Ethan's girls anymore. He's coming to work in the store with me and that's it. Who cares about his girls? My only concern right now is whether he will like this guitar. He needs something to teach classes. Ethan Winston at my shop, teaching classes. That should definitely keep the store from going under. Oh well, if he doesn't like this guitar, he can buy another one when he makes his own money.

On my way to the back room I see the two of them sitting in Charlie's car. It's a bit chilling...Ethan keeps showing me sides of him that I haven't seen before. Usually he's all smiles and charm. All the girls he charmed and he never noticed me watching him.

I find a case for the guitar and open it. As I carefully set the guitar inside the case, I hear my dad's voice. "Follow your heart my little girl, follow your heart, my girlie girl."

A tear forms in the corner of my eye. My dad used to pick me up and spin me around. Then he'd set me down and watch me do the "penguin walk" because I was so dizzy. And he'd say, "Follow your heart, my little girl, follow your heart...my girlie girl." I'd close my eyes...and just feel...and somehow...I'd always find my dad. He was taken from me too soon...so was my mom. I miss them so much but could never tell anyone. Not Grandma, not Charlie. Grandma was stressed out about her store going under. Charlie was worried about Grandma. I buried myself in work and taught classes mindlessly to the point I even thought I lost my love for music. And then Ethan Winston sits in front of my building. And I hate him. I hate who he's become. Go back and be a womanizer, a rich kid; go back to the family that nearly destroyed my grandma's business.

"She a beauty," it's Ethan's voice behind me. "Someone just bought her?"

I close my eyes and take a deep breath. "Another rule: Stop sneaking up on me. Can't you knock or something?"

"Charity," he says. "The door's open."

"The store needs someone who understands music theory a little more than me," I turn on my heels and face him. "Everyone knows you're some kind of a prodigy...do you think you can teach classes here?"

Is he even listening to me? He's paying way too much attention to that guitar. The way he's touching it. If that's how he touches a guitar, I wonder how he touches a girl. What? A girl has to be honest...and curious...

"They lied about me," he says, his fingertips lingering on the guitar. "I'm no prodigy. But I'd be happy to work for you if you would hire me. I can teach, clean, sales, you name it, I've been in love with this place since I was a kid."

There goes that word again. "Love." He uses it so much and so easily I wonder if he takes it seriously. And I've been in this store since I was a kid. How the hell does he not recognize me? I had different hair back in college, and colored contacts. Oh and I was...pale. But not unrecognizable. I think.

"The salary's really low—" I'm really trying to sound apologetic and sincere to him but the way he looks at that guitar...I think I'm jealous. "I'm sorry, I owe the bank a lot of money."

Finally, he looks at me. That serious eye contact again. If he kisses me I will punch him. Please give me a reason to punch him.

"Can I crash here at night? Just a blanket on the floor will be fine. I'll do whatever you need me to do. I've lost everything. My shoes were taken in a fight...thanks for your flip flops." He's talking to me, explaining everything, and all I see are his lips. I hope my face looks serious. I almost have this urge to hug him...

"You'd rather sleep on the floor here than on my couch? Or, Charlie's ranch has a real bedroom if you want."

The two of us are in a small space, a guitar behind me. Ethan and I are facing each other. Charlie is outside; I know he's somewhere listening...

"No, no, I just...I don't want you to feel uncomfortable... or for other people to talk about you," Ethan reaches out and touches my cheek.

I regret what I said. I don't want him to kiss me. I want his hand off of me right now. Right now right now right now. But I'm not moving...

"Another rule: Don't touch me," I say and turn away from him. "It's not like you worried about how people would talk about the girls you've slept with."

"I liked someone...for a really long time," he says.

I can't see him but I just know he has that look on his face. I need to learn how to stay away from those puppy eyes

Shut Up and Kiss Me

If I'm going to work with him.

"My dad had me pretty booked with piano and violin practice, or recitals...I didn't exactly have time to go sleeping around," he says. "But...somehow I don't think you'd believe me."

And he's right. I don't believe him. Why would all these girls just claim they've slept with him? It wasn't just one girl or two. It was like a hundred. In a town like this, that's like every girl!

"You shouldn't have to care whether I believe you or not," I close the guitar case and hand it to him. "You're gonna be teaching classes here; try not to sleep with the students."

I squeeze myself out of that room and get as far away from him as possible.

Charlie stops me at the front counter. "You know your grandmother loved him, right? She used to say, 'The boy plays music with his heart and soul. Too bad his father's the devil.'"

I grab a seat on my favorite bar stool and spin left to right. "So why did she keep me from him every time he came into the store?"

"She knew you were obsessed with him! But you kids and your face...what...book? And the girls from the music school always blabbering something in your ears about that poor boy."

I look at Charlie and then towards the hallway. Charlie nods and mumbles, "Give my boy a chance..."

I walk to the backroom and Ethan isn't there. From one

Shut Up and Kiss Me

of the empty classrooms I hear the strum of a guitar. It's my song. I find him sitting on the floor in the classroom.

"If I could hold you tight...I'd show you how brightly you shine..." he's singing my song. I refrain from singing with him. We all know what happened the last time. The melody changed a little bit. Then a completely different chord.

"Girlie girl you been on my mind all day," he sings. "There's a lot of things I cannot explain...can I have a chance to show you the scars...a chance to show you...who I really am."

He's looking at the wall; I'm looking at my shoes. My shoes...my toes aren't poking out anymore. No wonder I'm walking funny today.

"Did you do something to my shoes?"

"I don't have money to buy you new ones...yet...so I fixed them for you. I'm sorry."

The guitar strumming relaxes us, I think. Or else we'd kill each other. He keeps strumming the guitar, which is a good thing. He's smart not to stop.

"Tell me about Veronica..." the question that's been on my mind for years finally finds the courage to come out.

"There was a girl at school...her name's Rachel. Just an unbelievably amazing girl. I really liked her. And my dad knew...." Ethan answers.

"Hey stupid, I said tell me about Veronica..."

"One day I left a note in Rachel's locker, saying that I'd wait for her in Musical Healings every Friday for three

Shut Up and Kiss Me 36

months. I'd like to have coffee with her or something. She never came."

I know about Rachel. Everyone knew about Rachel. She's the vocalist who always got embarrassed by Dean Winston. He told her that she had no talent whatsoever and the poor girl ran off the stage. Truth be told, she was good! And there were rumors about Ethan and Rachel. But...there were rumors about Ethan and a lot of girls. Is he really going to make me ask about Veronica...again?

"You really want to hear about Veronica?" Ethan sings.

I roll my eyes. Ok. I'll play. "Yeah," I hold a note. "I do..."

"Wow," he looks at me wide-eyed and keeps strumming. Then the music gets softer and softer.

"She was a nice girl," he says. "Encouraged me. Looked at me like I was somebody special. I needed that...badly."

He's joking with me, right? The entire town looks at him like he's somebody special. I have been watching him since I was in elementary school! I really want to hit him upside the head right now. But no, I will be a lady. I will be sophisticated. I will take a deep breath and remember that he works with me.

"Did you...?" I ask. "And don't you dare lie to me. I know where you're sleeping tonight."

"No, I didn't sleep with her. Contrary to popular belief, I haven't slept with that many girls."

But he *has* slept with someone. In this day and age, who hasn't? I've been tempted a few times. Just never got around to actually doing it.

Shut Up and Kiss Me

"Is this guitar...mine?" Ethan asks.

"I can only pay you a hundred bucks a week...so, I was hoping this guitar would make up for it. If you do well here, I'm sure I'd be able to pay you more in the future, but right now, this is all I can afford. I'm sorry..." This time I'm blushing. I really am. A music teacher for a hundred bucks a week is just ridiculous.

Ethan sets the guitar down. I won't blame him if he turns down my offer. He moves in closer to me. I swear he looks like a smiling Husky sometimes. If he licks me, oh my god, I will do so much more than punch him. He brushes his hair aside and I see a tiny little scar on his forehead.

"My old guitar, Misery," he says, then he shows me the piece of wood hanging on the string around his neck. "Misery, meet Charity."

He takes off his necklace and puts it around my neck. Rude, really, he doesn't even ask me if it's ok to do it, he just does it. Oh well, since he did it, I'm keeping it.

We sit in the classroom, completely silent, for about three minutes. That clock is moving really slowly...I think at the two minute, fifty-five-second mark Ethan makes an attempt to hold my hand. Then Charlie's voice calls out from the front and we both rush out. Thank you, Charlie. Perfect timing.

When we get to the apartment it is almost eleven o'clock at night. Charlie bought us dinner. I watch Ethan put his guitar next to mine in the living room. He sits down on the couch and crosses his fingers.

"Couch is half empty..." Ethan says.

"I'm kinda tired." Another big fat lie.

Shut Up and Kiss Me

His eyes follow me to my room. A little dumb looking, but I'll admit it, a little cute.

"Ethan, can you help me with something?"

Oh god, did I just say that? Lame! I hear footsteps...okay I need to find something I need help with. Water bottle! I unscrew the top and spill water on the floor.

"May I?" Ethan stands at my door.

I nod. He grabs a towel hanging on the door and wipes my floor.

"Sorry, I took out my contacts and can't really see."

He smirks, "Blind Charity..." He messes with my hair. I stick my tongue out at him. He smiles. I like it when he smiles at me like that. It's genuine, as if only I can make him happy.

Can I make him happy?

"What are you thinking about?" he asks.

"Nothing."

He reaches out to touch my forehead, I guess he already forgot about our rules. Doesn't matter I guess. I have to work with him, so I should learn to accept his flaws. I look up to see that he has one finger on my forehead and I smile.

"What are you doing?" I ask.

His finger travels down in a slow motion, tracing the bridge of my nose to my lips and down to my chin.

"You assume that I want to sleep with you..." his finger lingers on my chin, "but this mask is the only thing I want to

Shut Up and Kiss Me

take off."

In that moment, I realize what my dad said about following my heart. It's a different kind of beat. It's that look in Ethan's eyes that makes me feel as if I'm the only one in the world. It may be that this one night will be all that we share together or maybe tonight is the beginning of the rest of our lives. I don't know…and…maybe…I don't care anymore. I don't want to be stuck in cycle of maybe this, maybe that.

"Can you close the door?"

"Sure."

He walks to the door. And he keeps walking. What is he doing? Oh my god is he stupid? The door closes. I change quickly into a long t-shirt. This is sexy right? I mess up my hair a bit, look in the mirror and try different smiles and pouts.

What the hell am I doing?

I open my bedroom door and the lights are already off. Thank god for the little night light in the living room. Ethan sits up on the couch and looks at me, following my every move with his eyes. Usually when guys look at me like that I feel disgusted. But when he does it…it feels ok I guess.

"Need to go to the bathroom? I can get the lights for you."

"Nope, I'm fine."

I pull the night light from the wall plug. Bad idea. Now I really am blind. I feel my way around the room. Ethan giggles. Ok, that's his feet. Apparently he's ticklish. Duly noted. I sit on the couch and he scoots over to give me more room.

Shut Up and Kiss Me 40

"Wanna watch a movie or something?" Ethan's voice echoes in the darkness.

I turn to look at him and I can kind of see his figure in the dark. I try to be quick and smooth. He flinches a bit. I think I accidently hit his nose...

"Sorry," I say as I finally find his arm in the dark and lay my head on it. I feel as if there's a sound effect playing. Nope, that's his heartbeat. I can hear it clearly. Or is it my heartbeat? He inches closer to me slowly and wraps his other arm around me. This is different from any hugs I've ever had. Now I'm just waiting. After he kisses me, I'll punch him in the morning.

"Girlie girl..."

"Hmmm?"

"You don't wear contacts..."

"Shut up and kiss me."

LOVE WAS IN THE LOST AND FOUND

The coffee grinder whirls. There is a thud against the wooden cabinet, followed by a click and the aroma of fresh coffee drifts forward. These things usually interest Charity. Not today. Even the "Say YES" on the wall annoys her. She puffs out a breath of air and lays her head on her friend's shoulder. *It would be highly appreciated if the five people ahead of us would somehow remember they have somewhere to be and just leave*, Charity thinks. The woman making the coffee, Rose, sees them and her face brightens.

Charity forces a smile. She just wants her coffee. She doesn't want to buy Ethan cookies today, those chocolate chip cookies that he always tries to share with her. She wishes someone can make decisions for her; she wants her mind to stop thinking of what ifs. *What if he cheats? What if he leaves? What if what if what if!*

"The usual for my Charity and cookies for the Winston boy, yes?" Rose holds Charity's hand in hers. "Is that Lin Lin hiding behind you?"

The girl behind Charity steps up to the counter and stands on her tip toes to give Rose a kiss on the cheek.

"Our usual," Linda says. "And hold the cookies, we'll be here for a while."

Charity taps her fingers on the countertop. Guess she's getting Ethan cookies today. Linda decided. Good to have Linda around. Charity feels Rose's tender touch on her forearm.

"Something wrong with my baby girl today?" Rose's deep, ocean blue eyes shine with concern.

"Girl problems...you know," Linda reaches out and pats Rose's hand. "You look so good! Still glowing like the sun."

Rose's eyes shift from Charity to Linda, "I haven't seen you two together since...where did you go Lin Lin? Spain? England?"

"I went all over Europe," Linda flips her hair.

"Here is your coffee," Rose sets two mugs down on the tray. "Don't be a stranger now, you hear? Before you leave, you best give this old lady some sugar!"

Charity picks up the mugs and makes a beeline for the nearly hidden nook in the back of the coffee shop. Linda looks back at Rose and blows a kiss. Charity stops at a table with a "reserved" sign and sets the mugs down. Two teddy bears occupy the armchairs. She picks them up and sets them neatly in the basket next to the table.

"Our seats!" Linda twirls the "reserved" sign in the air before tossing it into the basket. "Don't tell me Rose leaves the bears there to..."

"I love her so much," Charity says. "She knows this has been my seat since forever and a day ago."

"Do you remember we had our first play date here?" Linda says. "How long ago was it? Kindergarten? Our parents sat right over there." She points to a table not five feet away. Charity tears a piece of tissue into little shreds.

"Sorry..." Linda lowers her head and sips her coffee.

"Smell that?" Charity closes her eyes and takes a deep breath. "Rose is baking fresh cookies again."

Love was in the Lost and Found

"You finally started eating cookies again?" Linda asks

"The cookies are for Ethan..."

"Couples fight..." Linda sits back and crosses her legs. "The first one's the worst, because you never think it could happen and when it does, you're like what the..."

Charity looks past the empty tables and out into the parking lot. Ethan drove today, in the car that Charlie had left him. Charlie had left him everything. His car, the money from selling his ranch and his book of songs. Just like that, he moved to Costa Rica for retirement.

Every week or so, Charlie would send an email, and it would always begin with, "An old dog can be taught new tricks huh! Even email!" Skype was a little too advanced and he just couldn't get the hang of it. She wishes she can send him an email and get a reply right away. He is a wise old man.

Linda holds her coffee mug in her palm and watches the surface of the coffee roll back and forth.

"Ethan didn't seem to recognize me a few minutes ago," Linda says. "I had to remind him we went to school together."

"He didn't recognize me five months ago either. I sat there in the street with him, every day for a whole two months."

"Wait what? Sitting on the streets? You wanna tell me the full story?"

"Another day, ok?" Charity says.

Linda brings the mug to her lips and sips like she savors the flavor, the taste of home.

Love was in the Lost and Found 45

"I remember every summer when you came to visit, you'd see Ethan and your eyes would just light up." Linda snickers. "What did you call him? Prince Ethan."

"Prince Ethan lives in my house now, sleeps in my bed, kisses my forehead every night and tells me he loves me," Charity sets her mug down and retreats into the pleasant protection of the chair. She wraps her arms around her knees and tries to remember the last time she was in this chair.

Her dad had gotten her some cookies and asked her to wait in the coffee shop while he went to pick up her mom. He had kissed her forehead and said, "Be good baby girl, Grandma will be done with classes soon if you want to go to her store instead. I love you." Charity was a high school senior and wanted to eat cookies and read gossip magazines. Answering dear old Dad with "I love you too" was just uncool.

A tear rolls down Charity's cheek as she holds herself tighter. *I love you too, Dad. I love Mom; I love you...I wish I had said something instead of eating those stupid cookies.*

"Only you can make that sound like a bad thing, Charity, only you," Linda says. "It's as if you've won the lottery, but you already have so much money you couldn't care less."

"And if I sleep with him...?" Charity gazes off into the air. "He would still do that?" She takes a bit of hair in her hand and counts the strands. If the number is even then she would sleep with him, if it's odd, well...let him wait. Two... four...six...but what if he loses patience like the others before him? He's already made it past three months, which is far longer than the others. Sixteen...seventeen.

Love was in the Lost and Found 46

"I don't even know if he looks at me as his girlfriend..." Charity says.

"Thanks. So I've been talking like an ass for the last three minutes and you just been zoning out huh?" Linda sneers.

"What? You said something?" Charity straightens herself up.

"You guys haven't slept together?" Linda leans forward and squints her eyes. "I always thought that given the chance, you'd jump on him."

"We sleep together. Just...no...you know..." Charity smears the coffee stain on her jeans.

Linda pushes her mug out of the way and folds her arms on the table. She stretches her eyes open, allowing the entirety of her dark chestnut pupils to tantalize Charity into spilling the beans.

"Nope," Linda says. "I don't know. I want all the juicy sexy dirty details."

Charity blushes and covers her mouth. There really aren't any juicy sexy dirty details. Even if there were, it's not something to be shared with friends. Is it? But the simple truth is, there aren't any details to share.

She mumbles, "We...kiss."

"And? A little touch here, a little kiss there, wow you still are a bad storyteller. You know how many stories I have to tell you? My god, I had some wild sex while I was in Europe." Linda closes her eyes for a moment.

"We have rules." Charity plants her feet on the floor. "He

Love was in the Lost and Found 47

can only kiss me." She takes the mug and traces its rim with her finger.

"Kisses...I like kisses..." Linda gently caresses Charity's forearm. "Kisses everywhere..."

Charity pulls away and returns to her position with her feet almost falling off of the edge of the cushion.

"No. Just kisses. No lower than my neck," she says.

"That trick still works?" Linda squeals. "I swear you're afraid of being turned on. Such a prude!"

Charity rubs her arms and tries to smooth out the hairs that stood up at Linda's touch. She says, "He's never been mad at me before. No... He has. Not like today though. He really blew up this morning."

"That man probably blew up several times when you're not looking. Oh geez, I think I feel sorry for him. How long have you been together? I go three dates and if the guy doesn't make a move, I do. Mama needs some loving."

Charity laughs and buries her face. "Don't mock me..." she mutters as she looks up in despair.

"Ok, ok," Linda gestures as if to zip her lips. "Tell me what happened today."

"I woke up to him kissing my forehead," Charity turns and fixates her eyes on Ethan's car outside. A handmade doll that she had made hangs on the rear view mirror. "He made breakfast, he's dressed and he got back in bed to wake me up."

"That's an 'I want morning sex' move, not 'wake up sleepy

Love was in the Lost and Found 48

face'." Linda cuts in while looking in the same direction as Charity.

"No, no, he does it almost every day. He always wakes up before the alarm."

"I'd wake up before the alarm too if my girlfriend gave me blue balls every night... What are you looking at? The tables are empty!"

Charity looks calmly over at Linda and stays silent.

Linda rolls her eyes. "Doesn't work on me Charity, I'm a bigger bitch than you are."

"Ok so anyway," Charity claps. "We were on our way out the door, and our neighbor also opened the door. I let go of his hand. Another rule is we don't hold hands in public."

Linda's eyebrows went up in unison and she mouths the words "What the f?" Then she mumbles, "A big f'ing f."

Charity ignores Linda's comment and keeps talking, "Then he just went cold. He pressed the elevator button so hard I thought he was going to break it. The drive here was silent. He didn't look at me and ask if I was cold, didn't kiss my cheek, didn't hold my hand, didn't put his hand on my lap. He just drove in silence. There wasn't even music. And he loves music. He just drove."

She pushes her hair behind her ears and hides her face between her knees.

Linda bounces up and walks over to Charity. "Let it out baby girl..." She shields Charity in her embrace. "Guys are such a-holes."

Love was in the Lost and Found

"I know I ask a lot of him," Charity pushes Linda away and returns to her curled up position in the chair.

"I know I can't compare to his girls. I just..." Charity sobs. "Have you seen Facebook? People post pictures of him and me and say that I'm his latest conquest. I'm not a fucking conquest!"

"I have his Facebook. He hasn't updated in forever. You don't post anything either. No pictures of him, nothing." Linda takes out her cell phone and scrolls on the screen. "But lots of nosy people talking about you two, yes. The perks of living in a small town I guess."

"He doesn't use Facebook...he doesn't have a phone yet. Says he doesn't need one. And he doesn't use my laptop either, I don't know why."

Charity looks at the handmade doll hanging on the rear view mirror in Ethan's car; it has two sisters. One in her car and another one somewhere in Costa Rica with Charlie. What would he do in a situation like this to calm Ethan down?

"How does he not have a phone? My ninety-year-old grandpa has a phone and posts on Facebook," Linda displays the screen for Charity to see.

"He was homeless for a little while..."

"Ok you gotta be shitting me! Tom Winston would not let his prodigal son wander the streets."

"It's how I found him, really," Charity says.

"Turned down the waterworks?" Linda asks.

Charity swallows a couple of breaths of air and nods.

Love was in the Lost and Found 50

"So basically...Ethan Winston has cut himself off from everyone. Everyone except you. No connections with anyone else?"

"He teaches classes at the store," Charity looks into her empty mug. How long has she been gone from the store? Is Ethan ok?

"A lot of students request him. His dad came a few a times too. One time he went with his dad somewhere, and when he got home he locked himself in the shower."

"I leave for a little bit and my most boring best friend has all these secrets she's been hiding from me!" Linda stands up. "Come on, take me back to your shop. I want to talk to Wonder Boy."

Linda skips happily toward the counter. Charity grabs the mugs and trails behind her. Linda veers left at the pastry display and pushes her way through the swing gate into the barista area. Rose beams a smile at Linda and hands her a cookie; Linda opens her mouth and takes a bite instead. Rose chuckles.

"Why the puffy eyes sweetheart?" Rose tilts her head and watches Charity as she strolls up to the front of the counter. "Did that Winston boy do something? I can hold back his cookies today if you want." The aging lines around her eyes only adds to the tenderness of her concern.

Charity shakes her head and says, "I just haven't sat in that chair in long time. A lot of memories."

"Those chairs are reserved for you any time!" Rose said. "Maybe next time you and the Winston boy can dine in instead of taking your coffee to go. The way that boy looks

Love was in the Lost and Found 51

at you, sweetheart, not a lot of men these days look at their women like that. Nowadays men come in holding hands with women and still turn and look at other women!"

The corners of Charity's mouth curl up and she says, "He just...landed on my doorstep."

Linda lays her head on Rose's shoulder and whispers, "And they're not doing it!"

"Lin Lin!" Roses gasps. "Young lady!"

Linda looks left and right before hopping onto the counter and sliding her butt across to the other side. Her feet land with a small thump and she shakes her butt at Rose.

A wholehearted laugh burst out of Rose and she lifts a paper bag in the air, "You girls bring the poor boy some cookies alright? Tell him these are fresh and made with love."

Charity accepts the cookies and nods. Let Ethan have his cookies. Linda is right. He doesn't have anything or anyone, except for her. It seems to be his choice to stay locked to her side. Maybe it's his right to be mad. Maybe cookies will make everything better. Please let the cookies make everything better. She's not good with apologies.

Linda waves goodbye to Rose and drags Charity out of the coffee shop as the door opens with its usual ding. Linda lowers her sunglasses from the top of her head and opens her arms to the blistering sun.

Charity dashes by a window that's been plastered with advertisements. A pair of eyes peer through and follow her movements. She halts at the door and takes a deep breath. Once inside, she snakes her way through the pianos on

Love was in the Lost and Found

display and the shelves of music sheets. She throws her arms around Ethan, sitting on a barstool behind the counter, nearly knocking him over. He steadies himself against the wall and catches her, his hands rest on her lower back. His eyes wander around. There's someone else in the store. He had seen the other girl follow Charity and the door dinged twice. Charity pulls him close and stops right before their lips touch. A hint of sorrow creeps its way into the hazel lining her pupils.

"Is it ok if I kiss..." Ethan's breath tickles Charity's lips.

Her fingers weave through the hair on the back of his head as she feels his lips against hers, the softness of the kiss sends a chill down her spine. His hands begin to slip from her waist and she pulls them back.

"Somebody's watching..." he stammers between kisses.

She clasps her hands around him as their lips part. The soft glow in his eyes draws her in as she whispers, "I don't care."

Click. Click. Click. Click. Click.

"Charity, jump on him or something," Linda continues taking pictures. "You're so getting tagged for this. This is a historical moment."

"Linda Stefania Chipley!" Charity spins around and stomps her feet. "I swear if those pictures end up on Facebook!" Ethan pulls her back and enfolds her from behind. She feels the tiny stubbles on his chin against her skin and she tilts her head for another kiss. This time, she blocks their faces with her hand.

"Oops. Tagged and...posted!" Linda smirks. "And that

Love was in the Lost and Found 53

is how mama does it. Now hurry up and change your relationship status."

Neither Ethan nor Charity answers. Linda turns her back against them and grins.

• • •

Linda wanders around the store. Not much has changed. From what she remembers from Granny Nash's stories, the place used to be a daycare center. The counter sits at the far left end of the store, leading to the classrooms in the back. Customers are greeted by a small selection of pianos and keyboards right as they walk through the door. The wall of accomplishments act as a backdrop to the instruments. A person idling around can look at pictures of the employees, their accomplishments and certificates. The majority of the wall is dedicated to the students, showcasing their triumphs and memories from their classes and recitals.

Linda gawks at Charity's picture and chuckles. It must have been changed recently. A few years ago, the picture showcased a morbid girl with black hair and green eyes. One summer Charity came to visit and never left. By the beginning of her senior year in high school, her hair had gone from blond to black and her eyes from brown to green. Most contact lenses would have looked "natural" but she went out of her way to buy the creepy looking ones. She had unhealthy sunken cheeks and it seemed like she didn't walk; she glided. Give her a violin or a cello though, she would give you a show.

The picture on the wall now shows a brunette with hints of red gleaming through her hair, velvety brown eyes and a sweet, almost childish smile. Linda deliberately skips over

Love was in the Lost and Found 54

Ethan's picture; everyone knows Ethan Winston. He has always been known as "The Wonder Boy," "The Prodigal Son," the guy that never places second in anything. She glances over at Granny Nash's picture and lowers her head.

"I'm sorry I missed your funeral," Linda whispers. "Don't worry about Ci...Charity. I'll kill that boy if he hurts her!"

Her eyes drift onto the violins displayed on the wall as her feet follow the directions. The aroma takes her by surprise, it's a sweet smell of natural wood, not musk from collected dust. This impresses her. Charity had never been good at cleaning. A book-sized plaque is on display in the space below the violins. The gold scripted letters read "Honorary Award." The recipient of the award, Cecilia Brooks, cello soloist of the Winston Orchestra. That's a name that only exists in Linda's memories. She hasn't heard that name since they graduated. Though the Winston Orchestra does bring back a few rather amusing memories.

Linda takes a few steps back and stands next to the only cello in the entire store. It belonged to Cecilia Brooks and it stands in the middle of an arrangement of rustic wooden chairs. She brushes her hand against the cello and reminisces on the captivating music she used to hear.

Oddly enough, behind the chairs is a bar table that stretches to the far end of the store, along with some stools spread out underneath. Granny Nash used to say that she tutored students at this very table to make money to get her own store. Her husband had tried numerous times to convince her to get rid of the "unfitting furniture," but to her, it was the foundation of the store. Linda giggles as she hops onto a stool and pretends she's looking out for her mom's car. She taps her fingers on the tabletop and sways to the

Love was in the Lost and Found

music she used to play with Granny Nash.

"Are you looking for the drawing?" Charity sneaks up behind Linda.

Linda lurches forward and yells, "What the hell?"

"We're even," Charity laughs. "The drawing's still there. Come and take a look."

"Does Ethan know who Cecilia Brooks is?" Linda follows Charity all the way to the end of the table.

"Yeah I showed him the yearbook," Charity stops at a spot and looks closely. "It's no wonder he didn't recognize me right? Should he have recognized me?"

"Have you shown him this?" Linda aims her phone at the tabletop doodle. "How old were we when we did this? And please...*I* didn't recognize you after graduation."

The nearly faded drawing shows four stick figures. Under examination, it appears to be two couples. "Ethan and Cici," and "Linda and Mr. Hottie" were etched underneath.

"I think we were eleven?" Charity rolls her eyes. "Do you think he would've liked Cici? You know...without the black hair and the green contacts and the ghostliness."

"Don't look back," Linda leans against the table on one arm. She looks at the array of guitars on the wall. Some of them had been there since before she left for Europe. "Is the store doing ok?"

"After Nana died, it was hard, there were just so much bills to pay. I almost had to sell the condo she left me," Charity picks at her fingers. "Charlie told me to think about closing the store, get what I can, and start a new life. Then I went home and found Ethan sleeping in front of my building."

"Some months later, the store is still here, that's good, right?" Linda says.

"I spent almost two months sitting with him in front of my building," Charity chuckles. "I wrote a song so that I could sing and do something."

Linda looks at Charity blankly.

Charity shrugs. "What else was I supposed to do? Leave him there?"

"Didn't you have things to do? Like...oh I don't know, teach classes here? Sell instruments? ANYTHING?"

"It wasn't a secret that Ethan was out in the streets. You know this town better than I do. But nobody helped him. For some reason he didn't come to the store to ask Charlie for help."

"Oh yeah! I remember now. The few times that Ethan's dad allowed him in here, he followed Charlie everywhere. I remember. Hey, you think Pretty Boy is getting lonely at the counter all by himself? Maybe you should go and lock lips with him." Linda kicks Charity's calf playfully.

"He's cleaning the shelves," Charity points in the opposite direction. Beyond the instruments on floor display, a few rows of black wooden shelves pave the way to the counter and the opening to the classrooms. "He has a schedule for cleaning the store. A schedule, Linda, a schedule.

"Good!" Linda hooks her arm with Charity's arm. "You suck at cleaning. You suck so bad that you would wipe off a

Love was in the Lost and Found

violin and there'd still be lint on it." They giggle and skip their way throughout the store to find Ethan.

"Cute butt," Linda says under her breath as she and Charity find Ethan with his head inside an open cabinet.

Charity squints at Linda and says, "Mine."

Linda smirks proudly and knocks rhythmically on the shelf. "Earth to lover boy, anyone in there?"

"These kids really like to mess up the music sheets..." Ethan backs up carefully and scratches his head.

"Oh! I forgot something!" Charity breaks into a run.

Linda races after Charity. Ethan inspects the area again before shutting the cabinet doors.

• • •

"Are those Mrs. Rosetti's cookies?" Ethan eyes the small paper bag in Charity's hand as he approaches the counter.

She dangles the bag in front of him, luring him behind the counter. She hands it to him with one hand and tugs on his shirt with the other.

He plants a kiss on her cheek and says, "I love you."

Charity pulls up a barstool in front of her and pats the cushion. He hops on and leans back against her. She wraps her arms around his body and clasps her hands together. The two of them spin left and right in sync.

Linda makes a disgusted face, "What's next? A choreographed dance?"

Ethan cocks his head sideways and looks at Linda, "Lin

Lin Chipley!" Ethan says. "The loud one! I had you confused with your cousin earlier."

"Pretty Boy Winston," Linda snaps back. "I see you're out from under daddy Winston's control."

"You look good," Ethan says. "Lost all that baby fat. I really didn't recognize you."

"Baby fat? Please. What do you want with my best friend?"

"Everything. Nothing. None of your business."

"Stop," Charity slaps Ethan's thigh.

"She started it!" Ethan rubs the spot.

Charity grasps Ethan's hand and their fingers intertwine. She rests her chin on his shoulder and stares off into the air. *He's mine...now. If he breaks my heart Linda will kill him for me.*

"You ok?" Ethan loosens his fingers a bit. Charity nods and nuzzles against his neck. He smiles and moves in for a kiss but stops himself. She reaches up and leaves a peck on his cheek.

Linda drums her hands on the counter, "Can I make a suggestion?"

"No," Ethan and Charity answer together.

"I'm just saying...close the shop and go home already."

"I can't close the store early. Where would you go?" Charity asks. "Come back here and sit!"

Linda peeks behind the counter. Another barstool with

pieces of its cushion missing stands by itself. "Is that Granny Nash's chair?"

"Yup," Charity says as Ethan attempts to make space for Linda to walk through. She tightens her grip around Ethan. Where's the line between healthy relationship and just plain creepy girlfriend? Linda squeezes through and hops onto the chair; it had always been her favorite. Granny Nash used to let the girls both sit in it and spin them until their hair looked like they had been on a roller coaster ride.

Ethan takes out a cookie, breaks it in half, and puts the other half back into the paper bag. He waves the small piece of cookie in front of Charity. She pouts and pulls away. He pushes the cookie a little closer to her lips. She takes a mini bite. He kisses her forehead and says, "I love you."

Linda widens her eyes as she watches Charity eat the cookie. Her fingers grip onto the cushion. She holds her breath and waits for Charity's response.

Ethan rubs Charity's arm gently and loosens himself out of her hold.

"Where you going?" Charity starts to reach for him but then retracts her arm.

"I'm going to eat my cookies..." Ethan lifts the paper bag in the air.

"I forgot. Sorry," Charity looks down at the counter.

Ethan smiles at Charity and reaches over the counter to mess with her hair. She bites her bottom lip as she follows Ethan to the door with her eyes. When the ding sound goes off, she walks over to the window and motions for Linda to join her.

Love was in the Lost and Found

"What's with him and the cookies? And you ate a cookie!" Linda pokes Charity's side. "Will you please answer the poor guy when he says he loves you? It's a little pathetic."

"Just watch what he does..." Charity says.

"Does he know why you don't eat the cookies anymore?"

"Lin...just...watch..."

Ethan sits down on the sidewalk and looks into the coffee shop.

"Have I been crazy all this time or is he looking at our seats?" Charity asks.

Linda stands on the barstool's footrest, tilting forward until the smooth glass touches her forehead. Charity pinches Linda's leg. "Don't be that obvious!"

Ethan takes out the half cookie and breaks it in half again. He eats the smaller pieces, one at a time.

"The way he eats his cookies..." Linda gasps.

"So it's not just me that sees this right?" Charity asks.

Linda looks at Charity and raises her eyebrows. Charity nods slowly. They both turn to watch Ethan again.

"When he first came to the store, I could only give him a hundred bucks a week for salary," Charity explains. "The day that he got paid, he went next door to buy cookies and..."

"Holy mother of cows!" Linda holds onto Charity's wrist, nails digging into her skin. "Is that...Rachel Hannigan? THE Rachel?"

"She's even prettier in person..." A chilling sensation

Love was in the Lost and Found

washes over her as Charity watches Rachel approach Ethan. He seems to be in a daze. She wonders what he is thinking about.

• • •

Ethan breaks the second cookie into halves. Then he breaks one of the halves into halves and pops a quarter of a cookie into his mouth. He looks at the teddy bears sitting at that table in the coffee shop. Back in elementary school, starting in late May, a little blond girl would sit in that seat with her friend. Every Tuesday, Wednesday and Thursday, Ethan would finish his piano class and see them sitting there, eating cookies and drinking whatever it was that they drank. It fascinated him that the blond had an odd way of eating cookies. She would first break the cookie into halves. Then only take one-half and break it into halves again. Then she would eat the quartered cookies, one at a time. He started doing it too, just to see what it felt like. While he waited for his mother to pick him up, he'd sit on the sidewalk and watch the little blond girl. She always sat with her feet propped up in the chair. She always hugged her knees. And she never left a single cookie crumb behind. By early August, she'd be gone. He would wait all year for the little blond girl to show up again.

The second year, he saw the little girl exactly nineteen times. His father had changed his piano teacher and he wasn't allowed to go to Musical Healing for lessons anymore. The next time he had those cookies again, it was in high school. The little blond girl's table was taken over by teddy bears and Musical Healing didn't feel so welcome as it used to.

"You really love those cookies," a familiar voice brings

Ethan out of his daze. Rays beaming from behind her pierce his eyes and all he can see is a dark figure. She lowers herself to come face to face with him. "Hi Ethan."

Ethan scoots back on the sidewalk, his shorts chafing against the hot concrete. Charity is going to be so mad about the shorts...

"Hi...Rachel..." He scratches his head and looks back at the Musical Healing store window. Charity and Linda are nowhere in sight.

"You're teaching, right? At this store? Musical Healing... why does that sound familiar?" Rachel sees Charity eying her from inside the store. Another person pops up, another familiar face. "They went to our school."

Ethan turns to see Charity and Linda standing by the window. "You recognize them? How? Lin Lin Chipley looks like a different person now."

"Small town, small music school, us girls were always in the same classes and buses; besides, it's a girl thing," Rachel says while keeping her eyes on the girls through the window. "What's the other girl's name?"

"Charity Owens, my girlfriend," Ethan stands up and wipes his hands on his shirt. That is another thing Charity will kill me for... "I think she's my girlfriend...we live together...well, actually, I live with her. Her grandmother owned the store. You remember Matilda Nash?"

Rachel nods.

"I don't remember anyone named Charity though," she says.

Love was in the Lost and Found 63

"Yeah, she legally changed her name after her grandmother died, it used to be Cecilia Brooks."

"That's Cecilia Brooks? I thought she was someone else from school, some girl named Veronica?"

"Yeah! I remember Veronica! I think she got married and moved...I don't know. Charity showed me a yearbook and I was like whoa! I been looking at her face for...whatever fifty-eight plus eighty-six days is...and I just really can't put the two together. It's like night and day."

"You with your numbers," Rachel giggles. "So are we going to stand out here all day or is my new coach going to introduce me to the classes I'm about to buy?"

Ethan blinks a few times. "Coach?"

"Let's talk inside."

He walks to the door and holds it open for her. She steps back and says, "I'll follow you." He stares down at the floor and shuffles his way to the front of the store. Charity meets him right at the opening and pulls him behind the counter. Their fingers clasp together and he lets out a sigh of relief. Charity smiles at Rachel as she strolls up.

"Charity, right?" Rachel asks and extends her hand. "Pleasure. I'm Rachel Hannigan."

"I know who you are," Charity shakes Rachel's hand. "Your YouTube videos are absolutely incredible."

"Thanks," Rachel grins and looks at the laminated class schedules taped to the countertop. She looks up at Charity and then the wall.

Love was in the Lost and Found 64

Linda holds on to the edge of the counter and pulls herself closer.

"Interested in classes? You sing, play guitar, piano... hmmm...Charity is an excellent violin teacher," Linda says.

"Thanks Lin Lin, good to know you still remember me." Rachel looks at Linda and then directs her attention to Ethan. "Actually, I need a songwriter."

Charity's grip tightens. *You had your chance...* Ethan's hand flinches. She loosens her grip. He turns slightly to look at her, eying her, as if asking if she's ok. She looks down at her shoes and a suddenly everything feels ok. Those shoes were eighty-dollars and Ethan had bought them for her with his first paycheck.

"But your songs are good," Ethan says. "People pay to hear you sing, no? At uh...Fire something..."

"Fiesta, yes, I sing there," Rachel looks through her purse.

Ethan looks down and sees that Linda is kicking Charity's foot. They both glance at her.

Linda mouths the word "rich" and rolls her eyes. Charity giggles.

"I know where it is," Ethan says. "I spent two days sleeping behind the restaurant. I gave the owner my phone in exchange for food. His son kicked my ass on the third day."

Rachel's hand stops in her purse. She stares at the class schedules. "I had no idea...I'm so sorry."

"Fiesta—isn't that Mateo Perez's dad's place? He used to throw parties there all the time," Linda says.

Love was in the Lost and Found

"That's...my ex-boyfriend," Rachel keeps her eyes on the schedules.

"Good that you dumped him. He's a douchebag," Linda says.

Charity and Ethan look at each other. Then they remember, yes, Linda has always been like this.

"So how can we help?" Charity asks.

Rachel looks up at Charity, then at Ethan, and then back to Charity. "There is an agent who is interested in signing me."

Ethan looks down at his toes. He wiggles his right big toe and then the left big toe, like they're having conversations with each other. Charity always laughs when he does that. No laughter today.

Rachel brushes her black bangs to the side to reveal a set of hazel eyes. With her hair tied in a ponytail, her dimples are even more distinct. Ethan feels Charity's grip tighten. It's almost as if she's holding her breath, staring at Rachel. Linda's spinning annoys him. Rachel's smile is as captivating as it had ever been. Charity drops her head. Ethan wiggles his toes again, gently hinting her with his heel. She giggles and leans against him.

"I need someone to teach me how to write a song with feelings. And...your songs are way better than mine, Ethan. I still have your CDs," Rachel heaves a sigh.

"Lin, come help me in the back? I have students coming soon. I need to set up," Charity says. Linda's kicks against the wall echo behind the counter. Charity pulls her hand free and rubs Ethan's arm. She gives him a quick peck on the

Love was in the Lost and Found

cheek and walks towards the classrooms. He reaches for her hand and holds on.

She turns and smiles at him, "The kids are coming soon, don't worry, Linda can help me set up."

Linda follows, walking backwards and keeping her eyes on Rachel.

"I know it's weird for me to come ask you to teach me," Rachel says. "Can you please look at me?"

Ethan points to the bar table by the door, "I sat at that table and I waited for you. The least you could've done is show up and tell me to stop waiting."

"Look Ethan, I liked you, ok?" Rachel slams her hand on the counter." I really liked you."

"But you chose Mateo," Ethan picks at his fingers.

"I was singing at his dad's restaurant, I saw him every day, he's...he can be...sweet and charming...like you."

"You knew his reputation though, why would you do that to yourself?"

"He told me he was going to marry me."

"A girl like you doesn't make bad decisions like Mateo Perez."

"You sound like my mother."

"Are you still going to have a job?" Ethan finally looks at Rachel.

"The hostess doesn't sing very well. So, yes." Rachel places her business card on the counter. "But signing a

Love was in the Lost and Found

record deal...it's huge."

"I can't write songs with you if Charity's not ok with it," Ethan walks over to the hallway entrance. "I can't lose her."

"What if we all work together?"

"Can I have a few days to think it over? I have to talk to Charity about it..."

"Yeah, sure. You have my card, please call and let me know either way, ok?"

Ethan watches Rachel as she leaves the store. *What the hell did I get mad for? That happened years ago...*

• • •

In the fourth classroom down the hall, Charity and Linda finish setting up for class. Ethan still hasn't come to join them. Charity sprays a cleaner onto the white board and wipes it with a paper towel. Pieces of paper towel shreds land on the floor. She pushes harder and wipes faster.

Linda holds onto Charity's wrist to stop her, "She can't take him from you if you don't let her."

Charity plops down on the floor as tiny beads of tears trickle down her face, "She's really really pretty!"

Ethan rushes into the classroom. Linda glares at him. He kneels down next to Charity and wraps his arms around her.

"I'm sorry it took so long" he says.

She buries her face in his chest, tears drenching his shirt. He brushes her hair behind her ears and kisses her forehead.

Love was in the Lost and Found

"I wanna hear it," Charity sobs.

"I don't have any feelings for her anymore..." Ethan pats the back of Charity's head. "I swear to you...I even told her that I can't lose you."

"You kissed my forehead and you didn't say it."

Ethan's eyes fill with tears as he holds her tightly, leaving a trail of kisses from her forehead down to the bridge of her nose, her cheek and her lips.

"I love you, you silly girl. Now you're going to teach class all puffy-eyed and your students are going to kill me."

"My turn," Charity pulls Ethan lower and kisses his forehead. *I love you, Ethan Winston.*

"Can I stay like this for a while?" he asks. "My neck is gonna snap soon but this is oddly comfortable."

"Go outside with Linda! Can you believe that we almost forgot I had class today?" she laughs.

He lifts his head up and wipes her eyes with his hand, "I like it when you laugh like you don't care who hears you. And you cry...a lot...but it's really cute."

"I'm not good with words like you are," she says and holds onto his hand.

"You're really good at holding my hand, and I would love to hold your hand all throughout your class but, you need both hands to play the violin. I'll be outside ok?" he says and kisses her forehead. She closes her eyes and waits. "I love you."

• • •

Love was in the Lost and Found

Ethan and Linda decide to play Go Fish to pass the time while Charity's teaching class.

"Do you have any aces," Linda asks, looking at her hand with great intent. She was the queen of cards in middle school.

"Go fish," Ethan says.

"What did you say to Rachel?" Linda pulls a card from the deck. While Ethan had been busy apologizing to Charity, Linda had picked up Rachel's business card and tossed it in the trash.

"Do you have any eights?" Ethan asks. "I told Rachel I'm still pretty pissed about what she did to me but I'll talk to Charity and see if I can take on another project. I didn't tell Rachel this but...we could use the money."

Linda tosses two eights on the counter. Ethan collects them.

"Do you have any...hmmm...fours?"

Linda shakes her head. "Go fish. You know she loves you right?"

Ethan pulls a card from the deck. "Do you remember when we went on our high school graduation trip? The one time my dad didn't have a teacher chaperoning me."

"The cruise? Uhhh...sevens. The one when I got ridiculously drunk?"

"Lin Lin, you were always drunk. Fish."

Love was in the Lost and Found

"This is true, but go on..."

"You knocked on my door and told me that Rachel was waiting for me in the arcade, and right before I went there, you said, 'you know she loves you right?'"

Linda puts down her cards. Ethan does the same.

"That day, I asked Rachel to run away with me. I told her that I would do anything to be with her, and I gave her three CDs, all songs that I wrote for her. She took the CDs and said to me, 'Ethan, Lin Lin told me your dad would give me a second chance for the audition, do you really think he would?'"

Linda bites her nails and says, "I'm sorry...I was just a kid back then. And you were this...musical prodigy. And I thought you could've helped her...I didn't know...sorry."

Ethan picks up his cards. "Do you have any threes?"

Linda picks up her cards again and looks at her hand. "Fish. Any fives?"

"Fish. Any sixes?"

"I'm serious about Charity though...she really really loves you."

• • •

The door bell chimes, a few parents file in and saunter around the store while waiting for their children. One of them asks about a violin and Linda jumps to answer. A few minutes later children came running out of the classroom, each with a small violin case in hand.

Charity walks behind the kids as if herding them toward

Love was in the Lost and Found

their parents. Ethan heads to the backroom and gives Charity a quick peck on the cheek as he walks by. She holds onto his hand and tries to pull him back.

"It only takes a minute to clean the room. Go say goodbye to the parents," Ethan says.

Chatter and laughter fill the air as the students wander off in all directions searching for their parents. Charity waves goodbye to the kids and retreats to her spot behind the counter. Digging her heel into the floor, she gives it a slight a kick and the spinning begins. She closes her eyes and hears her dad's voice. "Follow your heart, girlie girl…"

The spinning comes to a sudden stop and she feels Ethan's arms tighten around her. She keeps her eyes closed and listens to the rhythm of his breathing, her fingertips tap along to the beat on his forearm. Her dad's voice repeats in her head, "Follow your heart, girlie girl…"

"Cici, you take credit cards right?" Linda's voice booms from the violin section.

"Yes, we can do payments too!" Charity yells. She reaches up and kisses Ethan's cheek. "I think maybe Linda should work here."

"Cici?" Ethan nuzzles against her.

"Oh it's a nickname my parents used to call me," Charity picks at her fingers. Ethan closes his hands around hers. She snuggles up against him and says, "Well…my parents and Linda. Don't call me Cici ok?"

He plants a big wet smooch on her forehead and says, "I love you, Charity Owens."

Love was in the Lost and Found 72

Linda walks up to the counter, violin in hand.

"Sold it." She blows Charity a kiss. "You two look like middle school kids who just learned how to kiss. It's disturbing, really. There are kids here you know."

"I'll go get the case," Ethan says and trails off.

"Who woulda known?" Linda says. "Pretty Boy Ethan is the acting janitor and bitch boy. I like it. You should keep him. Maybe find out if he's any good between the sheets too."

Charity laughs and covers her mouth, "He's not a janitor! Not a bitch boy either."

"But you do want to find out about his skills in bed..." Linda says under her breath as she writes the invoice. "You guys should really also get a computer sales system in here. Invoices are so last century."

Charity looks at the receipt. "Lin...do you want to work here? I haven't sold a violin in... I don't know how long and you did it in five minutes."

"Oh good, you didn't wait for me to ask for a job application, no base salary, ten percent of what I sell, ok?"

"I can't do that to you..."

"That's too damn bad. Oh wow, I have a job. Now I need clothes to look more professional. Do you want a slutty sexy salesperson or a good good girl?"

Charity spins in her chair. She looks at the stack of papers underneath the cash register. The money that her grandma owed the bank is almost all paid off, thanks to Charlie's money. Well, thanks to Ethan using the money that Charlie

Love was in the Lost and Found 73

had left him. Charlie had told Ethan, "Use it how you see fit my boy. I trust that you'll do the right thing."

Half the new students that signed up for classes are here for the Winston Boy. If Ethan recommends a guitar, someone will buy it. He won't admit it but even he knows his dad sends some business to the store.

With Ethan's recommendations, more and more people have signed up for Charity's string classes and even some vocal lessons. Apparently no one ever noticed her credentials on the wall. Didn't matter that she won awards or traveled with the Winston Orchestra, it only mattered that the son of Tom Winston is teaching classes at Musical Healing and just like that, business gets better and better. Had Charity known that, she would've gone looking for him a long time ago. But would her grandma have approved of it? That's a question that will never be answered. Ethan is here now and he's here to stay, no one can take him away. Not even Rachel Hannigan... Charity ruffles her hair and lets out a deep breath.

"You're spinning again..." Linda says, leaning on the counter. "Stop it. Just stop thinking."

"I don't know when I'll pay everything off..." Charity stares down at her shoes. "My grandma was really sick...but I promise..."

"Promise what? You'll have sex with me instead of paying me? Goody, take your clothes off. Right now. Quick, before Ethan comes back."

Charity laughs. Linda and her fantasies... No one but Charity knows that Linda really only had sex with two guys. They don't talk about it, of course.

Love was in the Lost and Found

"Ok boss, I start tomorrow. Mama needs some new clothes so off to the mall I go," Linda puts on her sunglasses and struts off. She stops half way to the door, turns and winks at Charity.

Charity smiles and waves. How did she ever become friends with a girl like that? Oh, right, they bumped into each other on the playground and Linda made a big fuss until Charity shared a quarter of a cookie with her.

The parking lot looks clear. Only a little more than an hour till the normal closing time. Ethan's probably cleaning all the classrooms again. He said his dad taught him that the appearance of a school is everything. "Straight and neat makes money." But cleaning almost every hour is just borderline obsessive. Charity feels around under the counter for the light switch and flips it off. She picks up the store phone and sets it on silent. The sign on the door has two sides. One side reads "Come in for a Musical Healing" the other says "Healing in Session...for the OWNERS." She flips the sign and takes a deep breath. She finds Ethan in the classroom at the end of the hall.

"Almost done?" Charity stands by the door and rests her arm on the frame. She's seen it in movies. This is what sexy girls do.

"Nothing's ever done," Ethan's head pops out from under one of the desks. He lays flat on the floor and looks up at her, "You ok? You seem a little different today..."

She kept her eyes on Ethan as she took small steps towards him. She remembers the first time she saw him in her grandma's store. She was only in elementary school and she used the shelves to play hide and seek with her mom.

Love was in the Lost and Found

Then there was a little boy who stood by his dad's side. He pointed to the guitars on the wall and there was a light in his eyes, like the guitars would just make his world complete. But his dad picked him up and sat him down on the piano bench. He had made a sad face but when he clicked a few keys he smiled again, and that light was still there. She sees that light in Ethan's eyes now whenever he looks at her. She kneels down next to him and wipes the dust from his forehead.

"Is there gum under the desk? Loose screw? What?" She asks.

"Spider webs. Nasty..." Ethan starts to wipe his hands on his shorts but stops and looks at Charity. "Sorry, I keep forgetting."

She brushes his hair back and leans forward, "Meet me in the backroom ok?" She leaves a kiss on his forehead and rushes out.

"Something wrong?" Ethan pushes himself off of the floor and hurries after Charity.

She darts down the hall and nearly slides into the backroom. With her back against the cabinet and her palms placed firmly on either sides of her, she pushes off with her feet. Instead of sitting on top of the cabinet like she had planned, she finds herself slipping to the floor in a matter of seconds.

Ethan breaks into a run when he sees Charity sitting on the floor in the back room.

"Linda, watch the store for us ok?" Ethan shouts out before shutting the door. "Are you hurt? Sit back and extend

Love was in the Lost and Found

your legs, you can still move, right?"

"I can't do anything right..." Charity hides her face between her knees and crosses her arms over the back of her head.

"Training for the Olympics or something?" Ethan peeks at the top shelf. "What do you need? I can go get a ladder if you want."

"I wanted to sit on the stupid thing, not hop on it..." Charity stands up and smoothes out her clothes.

Ethan inches forward one foot at a time until they are standing toe to toe. Charity watches their feet in amusement as she drags her feet back, following his lead. The waltz comes to a stop when her heels hit the wooden strip. His fingers gently grip either sides of her waist. She doesn't look up, she can't look up, all she feels is blood rushing to her cheeks. Within the blink of an eye, her feet are off the floor and she glides backwards on top of the cabinet. He closes in, the tip of his nose brushing against her cheek and he whispers, "Team work."

She rolls her eyes and pokes at his side until he breaks into laughter. It's been her ultimate weapon against "almost doing it" moments since she found out that he's ticklish.

"Why the rush to come and sit on this thing anyway?" Ethan's eyes wander around the small space. It reminds him of the janitor's closet at school, and it probably served the same purpose when the store was a daycare center. He shields Charity's head with his hand, in case the floating shelf above caves in and the guitar cases on it come crashing down.

Love was in the Lost and Found

"I just wanted to sit in here like this for a few moments," Charity locks her fingers around Ethan's waist.

Adjacent to the cabinet is a dirt-stained plastic container that holds the mop and broom. She looks up and notices cobwebs in the corner of the wall. "It's dirty and small and kinda stuffy but…it's where I used to hide whenever I missed my parents."

"I can clean it up and move all the stuff into one of the classrooms. A fresh coat of paint and maybe a new light, this can be your little…girl cave?" Ethan surveys the room with his eyes.

Charity loosens her grip and Ethan straightens up. She holds his face in her hands and pulls him close until the tips of their noses touch. His eyes light up and his lips part into a grin.

"I like the way you look at me," she thumbs over the stubble on his chin.

"I can totally have this room cleaned up and ready for paint before we leave today. Linda's still outside. She can keep you company," Ethan clears his throat and pulls back a bit.

"Linda went home and the store's closed," Charity says.

"Oh see, that changes everything," he presses against the wall behind her with one hand. Her lips quiver before they meet his firm yet tender kisses. She listens to his shallow quick breaths as she unbuttons his shirt. He retracts immediately and looks at her in awe.

"Maybe we should go home?" He lifts her hand up to his lips and kisses her fingertips. "Or…maybe we should stop?"

Love was in the Lost and Found 78

"We almost had our first kiss in this very room," Charity leads Ethan's hand underneath her shirt. His fingertips brush against her skin and trace their way along her spine. She reaches through his open shirt and slides her finger across a scar on his chest. "What happened here?"

"My dad..." he lowers his head.

She leaves a trail of kisses from his chin to the scar on his chest as she pulls the shirt off of him. A different scar on his waist catches her eye; he lifts her chin up and kisses her.

"After I got that scar, I didn't have a choice but to stay at your building. So in a way, it's a blessing." He wraps his arms around her and kisses the soft spot behind her ear, "I'll stay by your side as long as you let me."

"You're mine," she whispers. "I love you Ethan Winston. You're not allowed to leave, ever."

The normal air conditioning hum seems to have turned itself down today. The usual children's laughter coming from the park just beyond the classrooms' windows is nonexistent. The store's phone rang eleven times but was unable to make a sound. Pedestrians wander by on the sidewalk and look into the store. No lights, doors locked and a "store closed" sign welcomes curious eyes. As the sky blends into shades of gray, a yellow convertible pulls into the spot in front of the store, its wheels squeal to a halt.

Inside the back room, a couple lie on top of an open guitar bag that serves as an impromptu bed. Charity lays her head on Ethan's chest, feeling it rise and fall, his heart beat pumping drum-like rhythms into her ear. Ethan's fingers run

Love was in the Lost and Found

through her hair and she closes her eyes. Her forehead felt the warmth of his kiss.

"I love you," she says.

"I love you too," he smiles. "You ok?"

"A little sore..."

"I'm sorry..."

"No, it's ok. The way I heard it from my friends, I thought it was going to be excruciating," she says.

"The way I hear from my friends...oh wait...I don't have anything smart to say. So I'm just going to say I love you and I promise to be gentle next time."

Charity props herself up on one arm and covers Ethan's eyes with her free hand.

"If there is a next time," she says. She leans forward and kisses the tip of his nose and his chin.

Music blasts from the yellow convertible outside the store. A figure moves around in the car, searching for something. Pedestrians only give the person a quick glance before passing by.

Behind the closed door of the backroom, Charity rests her head on Ethan's chest and intertwines her leg between his.

"Are things going to change now that we're 'doing it'?" She asks.

Ethan bursts out in laughter. Charity sits up and turns away from him. He pulls her back down and holds her with both arms.

Love was in the Lost and Found

"I'm sorry," he says. "You're just really cute. I hope that if I change in any way, it's for the better, ok?"

"You're already laughing at me!" she pinches his arm.

"What you said was really cute!" he says and kisses her forehead. "I love you." He feels around for the guitar bag pocket, opens it and pulls out a pair of underwear, "How clean do you think this bag is?"

She looks at the saggy, oversized underwear in his hand and feels a wave of nausea wash over her. "I'll run to the bathroom and get cleaned up, then just pull my jeans on. I'm not wearing that."

He holds the granny panties up with both hands. "Can you...never wear this again?"

"I wasn't planning for today!" she blushes. "Those are... sex preventions."

"Yeah but...they didn't work," he runs his fingers down her inner thigh.

She stops his hand, "Food first. I'm hungry."

"Ah. So there is a next time."

Outside, the music from the car stops and the driver side door swings open. Bare feet land harshly on the ground and dash to the Musical Healing front door. Keys jingling, lock wiggles.

Charity sits up and looks around, covering her body with her arm. Then she sees it, hanging on the door knob, she reaches for it and suddenly she's down on the floor again, with Ethan's face less than half an inch away from hers.

Love was in the Lost and Found 81

"Three more kisses," he says.

"Three?" she locks hers fingers behind his neck.

He kisses her lips, "One." A kiss lands on the side of her waist, "Two." She felt the warmth of his tongue touch her thigh and she slaps his back. "Ouch! Three...well worth it I guess."

She sits up and turns away from him. "Help me get my bra, it's on the door handle. How did it get there?"

• • •

Finally, a click and the door opens. "Charity?" Linda yells out. "Are you here?" Linda runs through the store and checks behind the counter. Both Charity's cell phone and the store phone are on silent. She picks up the phone and dials a number.

"Rosetti's Place," a woman answers.

"Hey Rose, I'm in Charity's store, I don't see them up front, stay on the phone with me ok?"

"Oh sweet cheeks you shouldn't go in there alone! I'm sure nothing happened because it's been quiet all day but..."

Linda takes small, calculated steps towards the hallway. None of the lights in the classrooms are on.

• • •

"Girlie girl....do you hear something?" Ethan pulls on his shorts and helps Charity put on her shirt.

"No one's in the store but us," she holds his shirt so that he can put his arms through.

Love was in the Lost and Found 82

A loud knock sends them both jumping and looking at each other wide eyed. Ethan grabs a leather violin case from the cabinet and hides Charity behind him.

"Charity! Ethan!" Linda's voice roars through the door as the door knob jiggles. "Are you guys in there? Is everything ok?"

"My hero...with a violin case," Charity muffles a laugh. "We're in here! Stop knocking! You're gonna break my door!"

"What do we do now?" Ethan whispers. He puts down the violin case and buttons his shirt. He looks at Charity and fixes her hair. He's getting pretty good at it...that or she's just getting used to it. He gives her two small kisses. "Two and three."

She pulls on her jeans and stuffs her underwear in the back pocket.

"Here, get behind me," she says and switches places with him. He wraps his arms around her waist and picks her up. She giggles, "Stop! Act normal! Are you ready?" He nods and kisses the back of her head. She reaches out and turns the door knob.

The door creaks open as Linda's face slowly comes into view. She stomps forward and screams, "What the hell is wrong with you guys? Can't answer the damn phone? Someone saw the car outside but the store's closed and went and told Rose! And then she called the store, no answer. Charity's phone, no answer. So she called my mom. And my mom thought maybe Ethan murdered you so she called me."

"Lin...slow down," Charity pats Linda's arm. "I'm sorry...

Love was in the Lost and Found

it was only maybe an hour before the store's usual closing time, I didn't think it was a big deal. Sorry."

Linda looks at Ethan; he immediately drops his head. She then turns to face Charity and leans in closer to take a whiff. An ear-to-ear smile appears on Linda's face. She spins on her heel and walks out of the door.

"Hey Pretty Boy," her voice echoes within the hallway. "Your shirt's buttoned wrong dumbass! I'm gonna go next door to tell Rose you guys were in the back cleaning classrooms. You two...go home. Quit scaring the living hell out of everyone."

Charity turns around and looks at Ethan, "I think she knows..."

"Really?" He kisses her cheek. "I thought you kept your cool perfectly well."

"Let's go home, I'm so hungry."

"Give me a few minutes, I'll clean up here. I think that guitar bag is trash...or you wanna keep it? It's kind of a... keepsake?"

"If you keep the bag, you're never touching me again," Charity says. "Your choice."

Charity goes to turn the store phone back on while Ethan cleans up the back room. The phone rings in her hand, she sees the caller ID and wonders if she should pick up.

"Musical Healing, this is Charity," she picks up.

"Hi Charity, it's Rachel Hannigan, I was in your store earlier today."

Love was in the Lost and Found

What should Charity say? Or maybe she should just hang up. That'd get the point across. *Stay away from my boyfriend.*

"Hi...Rachel."

"I'll just get to the point," Rachel says. "I really need Ethan's help and I'm willing pay whatever you want to charge me. I've worked with other people and the thousands of dollars I spent showed no results."

Thousands of dollars...I can even buy Ethan a phone.

"Can I talk to Ethan about it tonight and get back to you?"

"Will you guys please think about it? I know he'd listen to you...I'll call you tomorrow."

Charity looks at the phone screen as the light dims. Ethan comes up behind her and tickles her. Her laughter fills the store as she leans against him and closes her eyes. "Forget cooking, let's just go out to eat."

"Whatever you want," Ethan kisses her cheek. "Something wrong? You keep looking at the phone."

She sets the phone back in its cradle and locks her fingers with his. "Promise me that you're completely over Rachel."

"Tell you a little secret," he whispers and kisses her earlobe.

She sucks in a breath of air and waits for him to tell her he loves her and he will always be there.

"There was another girl before Rachel," he says.

She drops his hands and turns to face him, her eyes

Love was in the Lost and Found 85

piercing through his, "Thanks, that's supposed to make me feel special?"

He rubs her arms gently, "Hey calm down...I love you." He locks her in his embrace and kisses her forehead. "I never actually met the girl, just caught glimpses of her. I was in elementary school and I only saw her during the summers, usually next door at Mrs. Rosetti's but there was one time I had caught a look or two at the park behind the store."

Charity feels a chill run down her spine. What do I say?

"First you wanted to know about Victoria, now you want to know about Rachel, but you have to realize...if there's anyone in this world that you should be afraid of, it's that little girl," Ethan says. "If I ever meet her, I'd want to introduce you to her. I'd tell her that when I was little, I'd wait for the moments to see her, I'd wait for summer to come so that I can see her, and I finally found someone who makes me feel the way she does."

"And how's that?" Charity's lips tremble.

Ethan looks out the window, smiles and then looks at Charity again. "Like I wouldn't care if the sky came crashing down, I'd have the strength to hold it up for her."

She pokes his chest repeatedly, "I went to that stupid school too you know? But you always had your eyes on Rachel."

"You transferred in during senior year, how was I supposed to just all of a sudden forget the girl I had a crush on? Did I notice you, of course I did. But...ok, I really liked Rachel. And to be fair, you looked really different back then. You had a different name and you didn't seem so...friendly."

Love was in the Lost and Found

"I had a lot of issues I was dealing with...of course I was different. You were a stupid drunk back then."

"So...can we let bygones be bygones?"

"No. I want to hear you say you're over Rachel."

Ethan chuckles and kisses Charity's forehead, "Absolutely one hundred percent over Rachel Hannigan."

Charity adds, "And absolutely ten thousand percent in love with Cecilia Charity Brooks aka Charity Owens."

"Are you a spy or something?"

"Say it."

"And one million percent head over heels in love with Cecilia Charity...Bruuhhh...Owens."

"Brooks. Brooks Owens."

"One billion percent head over heels totally crazy in love with Cecilia Charity Brooks Owens. And, and, wait for it...I'm keeping her forever."

Charity's hands slip into Ethan's back pockets. "I can't be your girlfriend forever."

"I know. You're gonna be my wife one day."

Wife...he said it first.

• • •

Sunlight streams through the window and a sweet aroma awakens Charity. She's snuggled comfortably under Ethan's arm. There is no point in blushing at their naked bodies under the sheets but she does anyway. His arm tightens around her and she feels his kiss on her forehead.

"Did I wake you?" she asks. "I'm sorry."

"French toast is on the bedside table," he says sleepily. "Shouldn't be cold yet...if they are I'll go heat them up for you."

She ruffles his hair and kisses his cheek.

"I love you," she says under her breath. As she sits up and wraps a blanket around her body, he slides closer to her and lays his head on her thigh. She sets the plate carefully on her lap, almost wanting to set it on his head. She cuts the toast into small pieces and asks, "You want a bite?"

He massages her thigh, "Can I take a bite of this instead?"

"After we eat...maybe."

Ethan pushes himself up on one arm and picks up a piece of toast with his fingers. Charity gives him a cold stare, "Don't use your fingers! They're probably dirty."

He looks right back at her, carefully lifting his hand to her lips. She accepts the toast and leans back against the headboard.

"One day you're gonna stop doing all this for me," she says. "And I'm gonna hate you."

If nothing lasts forever, then I might as well enjoy it while I can. She picks up a piece of toast with the fork and feeds him. He shakes his head. She forces him to eat it anyway. Her phone vibrates under the pillow. She hands the fork over to him and picks up the phone.

Love was in the Lost and Found

"You're up early," Charity says. Another piece of toast comes at her. She gladly accepts. "Yeah I completely forgot you have a key..." She picks up a piece of toast with her hand and feeds it to Ethan. He tries to bite her fingers. "Ok, ok, thanks. We'll see you at the store."

She tosses the phone to the side and dips her finger into the syrup.

"Your fingers might be dirty," Ethan says.

Charity drips syrup on his cheek and licks it off of him. "Linda's gonna open the store for us today."

He flips her over and sets the plate on the bedside table, "You did one, so I get to do one too."

"Did what?"

He pulls the blanket away and drops a piece of toast on her stomach. She breathes deep. He bites down on the toast, his teeth gently scraping against her skin, trailing drops of syrup till a soft kiss lands on her rib cage. The kisses travel back the same route, wiping off each drop. He wipes off the last drop with his finger and swabs it on her lips. She pulls him in and kisses him.

"Where have you been all my life?" Ethan holds himself up with his hands on either sides of Charity.

"A lot closer than you think," Charity lifts herself up to kiss his chin. "You just never noticed me." She bites his shoulder and he collapses onto the bed.

"I'll make it up to you," he turns and lies flat on his back, letting her rest her head on his chest.

Love was in the Lost and Found

"How?" Her fingertips dance across his chest.

There was a time when she was little, she walked into her parents' bedroom and she saw her mom doing that to her dad. She had asked her mom what she was doing and her mom had answered, "Daddy's chest is a big dance floor and only mommy's ten little dancers can dance on it."

"I'll stay by your side as long as you allow me to," Ethan lightly brushes Charity's hair.

"And what if that little girl from the coffee shop walks into your life?"

"Charity, haven't you noticed?"

"Noticed what?"

He pulls her on top of him. Charity feels her cheeks flush. She puts her hands on either side of him, then on his chest, then against the wall. Her head droops and she pouts. He smiles and holds her waist with his hands, sliding her backwards slowly until she is comfortably on top of him.

"You popped up out of nowhere and you conquered everything and everyone. If you want to leave one day, you're gonna have a really hard time getting rid of me," he says.

She lies there silently. He has an odd heartbeat, it's as if it beats twice and stops once. It literally skips a beat. Just like when he says something in total honesty, the pattern always skips a beat. This isn't one of his well-rehearsed lines. She knows he's telling the truth. She hears his sincerity. But why is it so hard to believe? How much has she known about him through the last few years and how much has he known about her? In such a short time he claims to be in love with her and she gave him the last thing that she held on to. So many things she's unsure of, so many stories she's still sorting out in her mind, but whenever he comes close all she wants to do is listen to that heart that skips a beat. Did it always skip? Or does it only skip for her? Does any of it matter?

"Ethan?"

"Yes, girlie girl?"

"You're not allowed to leave me." A drop of tear lands on Ethan's chest. "I know that I'll push, I'll always doubt if you're telling me the truth, and when you say you love me, I might not answer, but you're not allowed to stop saying you love me."

Ethan wraps both his arms around Charity and kisses her forehead.

"There go those tears again," he says in a sing-song tone, as if he's trying to find a melody. "Let it out girlie girl..." he whispers. Tears stream from her eyes.

"One word and I'll be here," the melody becomes a little clearer. Ethan starts to sing:

"Maybe these words others have heard before,
plenty of promises I broke...
and those broken promises led me to you.
No warnings at all, you came out of hiding and found me.
All the things that used to hurt now seem so small.
All the beauty that I've seen in this world can't measure
to how clearly I see your face.
You came you conquered, you gave me peace.
I'm perfectly fine alone...but better with you."

"Whether forever is written in the stars..." Charity sings.

Love was in the Lost and Found

"Sing it with me," Ethan pats Charity's head. "You got this."

"The future is something we cannot see," Charity sings.

"Together we explore destiny," Ethan sings.

"One word and I'll come find you."

"One word and I'll never leave."

"And if fate forces us apart..."

"One word..."

"Together we create destiny."

Ethan keeps humming while Charity dries her eyes. She suddenly sits up and his questioning eyes wander in her direction. She rummages through the drawer in the bedside table. The first box she picks up has the words Her Pleasure on it, she laughs and tosses it back. Finally, she feels the texture of paper and pen. She grabs the the pocket notebook and pen and hands them over to him.

"Better write that song down," she said and reaches out for Ethan's t-shirt on the floor.

He watches her as she slips on the shirt and walks out of the bedroom.

"One day I'm going to make Cecilia Charity Brooks Owens my wife," he writes in the notebook.

Charity stands in front of the vanity mirror and exhales. *Does it mean that things are "serious" now? Have we been dating for 3 months or 5? Or maybe we've been secretly in love with each other for our entire lives?* She strips off the

Love was in the Lost and Found

t-shirt and crumples it into a ball. If only she could make it into a stuffed animal of some sort. The smell of Ethan is all over it. Strange, she's never been the type of person to smell someone. It's not like he smells great it's just a scent that gives her a sense of security. *Isn't that a bit obsessive? A whiff of a man provides a blanket of soundness. Oh god Charity, get ahold of yourself! What's next? You're going to cling onto him for the rest of your life?*

After a quick shower, Charity wraps a towel around her body and peeks out the door. Ethan's dressed and plopped on the couch. *Mrs. Charity Winston, that doesn't sound too bad, right?* She tiptoes out of the bathroom and his head sticks up from the couch, his face half covered by a cushion and he looks like a spying pet. She strides into the room as if playing obstacle jumps and shuts the door. A sound of "Don't look!" is barely toned down by the door.

• • •

Ethan stretches out on the couch and covers his face with a cushion. "I love this girl," he laughs and kicks his feet.

The bedroom door swings open again and light pattering footsteps lead to the sound of sliding drawers. Charity has a tendency to pull too fast and one of the drawers usually makes a creak sound right before the whole thing comes off the rail.

Ethan rubs his palms together and waits for Charity to stomp her feet in place and tries not to spew any profanity. She does the cutest things. He has always heard from friends that have been in relationships for years that "the cuteness eventually becomes annoying."

Love was in the Lost and Found

So the goal is to remember how cute she is now and to find more cuteness as they grow. Something about this girl reminds him so much of the little girl from the coffee shop. He can't stop watching her, wanting to be near her. It happened the first time he saw Charity too, but at the time his mind was occupied on Rachel. What if he had asked Charity to go out for coffee instead of Rachel? She probably would've rejected him. Back in high school, Charity almost seemed...empty. The only time she seemed alive was when she was playing the cello. It was as if the music had taken over control of her body and she just entered a different dimension that no other human being could comprehend. Rachel was an excellent singer but Charity *felt* the music.

Fluttering papers hit the floor and Charity screams, "I'm going to toss this stupid...fuc...ugh!"

Ethan rolls off the couch and joins Charity in picking up the papers.

"I called it!" he tried to control his laugh. She slams the paper and pushes him to the floor. "That's pretty sexy," he sits back up and pulls her towards him.

"You can't replace it, remember? It belonged to your grandma," he rocks her back and forth.

"Stop rocking me," she said. "I'm not a baby."

"Sorry," he stops the rocking and eases his grip. He scoots back and begin collecting papers.

She heaves a sigh and covers her face.

Ethan keeps his head down and organizes the paper into a pile. The fallen drawer finds itself being pushed back into its place and a pile of papers stack in before it closes with force. Charity's hand snatches Ethan's calf before he can walk away.

He kneels next to her and brushes her hair away from her face; he says, "I'm not going anywhere." She tugs on the collar of his t-shirt and pulls him in for a kiss.

Her eyes glimmer with shame, "That's what you say now."

A gentle stroke of his palm cools her reddening cheek, "It's like I'm dating two girls. Some guys have to cheat for that to happen."

Her pursed lips part into a smile and she picks at her fingers. He sits and crosses his legs. Silence surrounds them as she picks at the carpet fibers and he taps his finger along to the ripping rhythm.

"I love you," she breaks the silence.

"Sometimes, I have nightmares," he responds. "That I wake up and all of this is gone. And then I feel you next to me and I'm sleeping in a bed, not on the concrete, and maybe right at the moment, it doesn't feel completely ok but it brings comfort, and that is enough."

Charity slides on the carpet floor and positions her legs on either sides of him. He tilts his head forward and she kisses his forehead.

"I'm more scared of losing you than anything else in this world," he says.

"You're the Winston Boy," she says. "Now that you're all cleaned up again, people are going to come find you. Rachel did..."

Love was in the Lost and Found

"I really really like your bed though…" Ethan gives her delicate kisses on her neck.

"Just my bed huh?"

"And you…I really really like you too. In fact, I kinda love you. Just a little bit."

• • •

Charity wipes her hands on his shirt and holds onto his shoulders to stand up. His hands slither to her backside, drawing her towards him. She squeals as he playfully squeezes her. She looks down at him as he rises up, one leg at a time. She wouldn't mind seeing him down on one knee again. It's a crazy thought. It's insane. *But isn't this what all the movies and great stories were about? Take a risk, live for the moment, marry the guy you've only known for three months.*

"It's been proven," he ruffles her hair.

"What?" she hates when he messes with her hair. But that's ok, it's an acceptable flaw.

"You are my rock, my foundation, my clutch," he says. "I couldn't get up off of the floor if it wasn't for your really nice butt."

She laughs and slips her hands into her back pocket. *I have a nice a butt.* A plastic card prevents her hand from comfortably settling in the pocket and she pulls it out.

"This is yours," she shows the bank debit card to Ethan. "You've made quite a bit more than two hundred dollars in the last couple of months and you told me to put it in the bank."

"A hundred a month is more than enough," he walks into the kitchen and opens the fridge. "All I get every day is cookies. It's your account anyway, you should keep it. I don't pay rent, utilities, bills, nothing. Want something to drink?"

"This is the account with what's left of Charlie's money so I put your paychecks in there. I don't get why you won't open a bank account."

Charity walks into the kitchen and leans back against the counter.

"Ok, let's stop at the bank before we go to the store," Ethan drinks juice directly from the half-gallon jug. "We can be ahead of their payment plan, bet their jaws will drop."

"No," Charity takes the empty jug from Ethan and covers his face with her hand. She has her temperamental moments. He doesn't like to drink from glasses. It's an even exchange. "We're going to the mall."

• • •

The automatic door to the mall entrance won't open for them. No matter how Charity and Ethan walk in front of it, wave their hands, even jump a bit, it just won't open. A toddler lets go of his mother's hand and stumbles towards the door. The mother instantly follows the child. As she takes hold of him, the door opens. Charity waves at the little boy. He drools.

"Thanks little man!" Ethan smiles at the boy. "Can I have a high five?"

"High five buddy," the mother says. "Come on, you can do it."

The boy lifts up his hand. "Good job!" Ethan laughs and gives the boy a high five.

The mother looks at Charity and says, "He will be a good father one day."

Charity smiles and nods. Ethan waves goodbye to the little boy and takes Charity's hand, "Is it ok?"

She locks her fingers with his, "It's more than ok."

The two of them saunter through the mall, hand in hand, singing along to songs blaring from the stores. She never knew anyone could actually do what she does: sing through a row of stores without stopping to think about what song it is. A neon sign advertising cell phones catches her eyes and she drags Ethan in the direction.

The selection of smart phones on display beam at him. There was a time that he could change phones as often as he pleased. His dad always insisted that he have the newest technology available.

"Tools of the trade," his dad called them. "How does one achieve greatness without proper equipment?"

A tear builds up behind Ethan's eye and he sniffles. He holds onto his side as he remembers the radiating pain from being kicked in the alley. He had traded his phone for food and a place to stay. He had a right to be there. Apparently the restaurant owner's son disagreed. Charity's soft touch on his arm brings him out of his daze.

"What's wrong?" her voice brings such comfort.

He shakes his head and steadies himself, "Nothing. Sorry...just...these are really nice phones huh?"

"My man Ethan," the salesperson approaches. "And he brought a pretty little lady!"

Charity's eyes widen and she holds onto Ethan. Ethan has friends? Of course Ethan has friends. Or is it a guy thing to be all buddy-buddy?

Ethan puts his arm around Charity, "Joel, good to see you man. This is Charity."

Joel looks down at Charity and reveals his pearly whites. "Hello hello little mama, what can I do for you love birds today?"

Charity looks up. Joel shouldn't be selling phones. His hands look like they could easily crush these phones by accident.

"I want to change my plan," Charity says. "I think my plan already ended anyway."

"Let me get your number and look it up right quick," Joel clicks around on his laptop. "Eh, Ethan, I'm not gonna go calling your girl alright? We good?"

"We good." Ethan laughs.

"You should get this phone," he says and shows Charity the phone he was looking at. "It comes with an app that's basically a simple recording studio on the go. Freaking blows my mind."

"You still got that taste, brother!" Joel says. "That phone is like the Lady Gaga of phones. Beautiful, top of the charts, and just a little freaky."

Charity looks at the description under the phone. One

Love was in the Lost and Found

ninety-nine with a two-year contact. She looks over at the free with two-year contract phones; one of those is plenty for her. She's not good with all this technology stuff anyway.

"So...the debit card, it's my account?" Ethan asks. "And you're sure you don't want me to pay the bank first?"

"I want you to buy something nice for yourself," Charity says. "We're all caught up with the bank, thanks to you."

"Joel, is she up for a new contract?"

"Dude, Ms. Dashing Charity Owens over here hasn't had a contract for like a whole two and a half years. I've changed five phones already," Joel adjusts his glasses.

"Good, I wanna buy this one for her," Ethan points to the phone that Joel referred to as the Lady Gaga phone.

"Ethan are you crazy? We came to the mall to get you a phone today, not me."

"Oh. See, you should've told me that. Oh well, guess you're getting a new phone too."

"We can do the family plan right?" Charity looks at Joel.

"Y'all can get the family plan, start a real family and come back to get a phone for the baby too." Joel hits Ethan's arm playfully. "I got a friend at the jewelry store, know what I mean?"

Charity blushes and looks down at her shoes. Ethan rubs her back and kisses her forehead.

"He's just kidding, don't worry." He looks over at the free phones in another section. She pulls him back to her side.

Love was in the Lost and Found

"Sorry, I forgot." he kisses her cheek. "I love you."

Charity smiles.

"Awww y'all make me wanna call my girl up and get all mushy mushy," Joel rubs his hands together. "But seriously, two phones yeah?"

"Yeah, I'm going to take a look at some of the free ones." Ethan says.

"No. Get the same phone as me," Charity says. "Or we both get free phones."

"Damn, Ethan, she feisty!" Joel drums his hands on the display case. "I like it!"

Ethan looks at the phone and lowers his head. Charity waits until Joel walks over to his laptop and then whispers into Ethan's ear, "There's not going to be another time that you trade your phone for food. I'm never letting you out of my sight."

He hugs her tightly and lifts her off the floor. She laughs and pats the back of his head. "I want the gold one. It's so pretty and Linda has one too. You?"

"You sure you don't got a little bit of black in your blood?" Joel walks back with a stack of papers in his hand. "You keep saying all these things that I'm just like wow shorty's reading my mind!"

"I'll take a white one," Ethan says. "It's different than the one I had."

As Charity and Ethan walk away from the kiosk, a muscular blond guy walks by and smiles at her. Ethan pulls

Love was in the Lost and Found 101

her closer to him and she slips her arm around his waist.

"He was just smiling at me…" she says.

"And I'm just a little cold, need you to keep me warm is all," Ethan says.

"Joel seems like he's known you for a long time…"

"Yeah, he has. My dad bought at least twenty something phones from him."

"Does he know about…"

"You know how I know I'm keeping you?"

"Enlighten me."

"My friends saw Facebook posts of me and didn't come looking. You spent 58 days with me outside your building."

"I could totally be one of those psychotic killers who's gonna murder you in your sleep."

"Please do it when you're naked. I'd like to die happy."

Charity takes the lead and drags Ethan into an electronics store. He looks at all the gadgets on display. All he has to do is go home and apologize to his dad and he can probably get his stuff.

"We could save the money and pay the bank…" he stops Charity in front of the revolving DVD shelf. "If I need this stuff, I'll just go home and get them."

She bumps him lightly with her shoulder and sticks her hand into his back pocket. "But I'm the kind of girl that really likes to spend her boyfriend's money."

"Well then girlie girl," he follows her lead Into the tablet computer section. "I'd give you the whole world if I could afford it."

Charity picks up the tablet that resembles the larger version of their new phones. The salesperson sees her and immediately changes his direction.

"This just came out last month," the salesperson says. "Danny" is his name. His piercing blue eyes seem to be looking at a particular place on Charity's body. "You can play with it. Go ahead, try it."

Charity swipes the screen and clicks around. The screen turns black. "Oops, sorry...here Ethan, you do it."

Ethan clicks the home button and opens the camera app.

"Smile," he says. Charity leans close to him and he takes the picture.

"It's great for videos, taking work on the go, pictures, so on so forth," Danny says. "Oh wow now I know where I've seen you guys!"

"Excuse me?" Ethan looks at Danny.

"You guys are friends with Lin Lin! She posted an event about you guys...some kind of music performance tomorrow."

"What performance?" Charity asks.

"I'm positive it's you guys, I remember thinking it's too bad the hot guy was kissing you. Lin Lin said it's a couple's performance and it's the first time ever."

Charity takes out her phone and dials the number to the store.

Love was in the Lost and Found

"Musical Healing, this is Lin-da! Can I book you for a seat for tomorrow's mini recital featuring our very Charity Owens and Ethan Winston?"

"Linda, what's this about a performance?" Charity asks. Ethan watches her with intent. "No I don't want to hear about it when I get to the store! I want to know NOW!"

Ethan takes Charity's hand and tries to drag her away. She doesn't budge.

"Ethan I'm going to buy that," Charity covers her phone and points to the item. "I want two please, Ethan can you choose the colors please?"

Danny faces Ethan with a big smile.

"What size do you want? The colors are all displayed here," Danny points to each item, keeping his eyes on Ethan.

"Hang on a second, I think she made a mistake," Ethan steps back and folds his arms.

Charity hangs up her phone and looks at Ethan, "Did you choose the colors?"

"Why are we buying two?" Ethan asks. "One for you is plenty...I have my phone."

"One's for the store, Linda sent me a bunch of information about using this as a sales system," Charity holds Ethan's hand and leans back against him. "Let me buy you one nice thing, please?"

His head starts to drop and she lifts his chin up, "Rachel is going to pay a lot of money for us to work with her...after we work with her, I'll use every single cent of your hard

Love was in the Lost and Found 104

earned money to pay the bank, ok?"

"We're working with Rachel?" he stares off into the air. "Shouldn't we discuss this first?"

"We did. You said you're over her. So, we can work with her, right?"

Ethan presses his lips together. Charity pulls his face closer and kisses his forehead. "I love you. I want to do this for us..."

"Yes, cutie pie, listen to your girlfriend! You guys want two? Oh and I'll so be at your show tomorrow!" Danny says.

"Did he just call me cutie pie?" Ethan mumbles.

"Ethan, you know these things better than me, can you choose?" Charity asks.

"Two sixteen gigabytes, both white, white is ok right?" Ethan looks at Charity. She nods and smiles.

• • •

As the store comes into view, Ethan and Charity see that the coffee shop's chalkboard stand is now standing in front of their store. "Charity Owens and Ethan Winston hand-in-hand music performance..." Ethan reads. "I guess you and I are performing something..."

"You're just going to do what Linda says?" Charity looks out the window. How long has it been since she's performed?

"I think it'd be good for business," Ethan says. "Besides, I want to play with you."

Love was in the Lost and Found

"You do play with me," Charity flips her hair and looks at Ethan.

He changes the gear to park and taps on the steering wheel. His face slowly turns red. He glances at her and immediately looks away. She slaps his arm. He reaches around her and pulls her close.

"We can play right now. In the car. Right here," he says.

"Linda knows we're here. She keeps looking at us. So creepy!" Charity says. "Wait outside for me ok? I'm going to run in and tell her that we're going to Rose's."

"I can just go get coffee for all of us, you go inside and sit."

"No. Just us," Charity unbuckles her seatbelt and opens the door.

Ethan gets out of the car and takes all the bags out from the backseat. He watches Charity run inside the door. She stops half way, she's screaming something. Linda walks towards her. *Oh no... Linda's joining us for coffee.*

"Take your phone and hand me the bags pretty boy," Linda stands by the door. "You two are not allowed in this store until lunch. Best bring mama something good to eat!"

"I'll set up my phone later," Ethan hands the bags over to Linda. Charity takes out her phone and hands it to Linda too. Linda smirks and walks back into the store.

"Come on, I want to show you something," Charity pulls Ethan by his arm.

"In Mrs. Rosetti's?"

Love was in the Lost and Found

The two of them walk into the coffee shop and Rose looks up. She wipes her hands and heads over to the coffee machine.

"Finally holding hands I see," Rose says.

Ethan scratches his head and says, "Hi, Mrs. Rosetti..."

"Two cookies for you sweetheart?" Rose sets down the milk can and wipes her hands on her apron. She grabs a tong and turns to face the tray of cookies behind her.

"Four cookies," Charity says.

Rose stops. She turns and looks at Charity. "The other two...for...you?"

Charity holds onto Ethan's hand, looks down at the floor and looks back up at Rose. "I think it's ok..."

Rose walks around the counter, comes face to face with Charity and hugs her. "Oh my sweet Cici...they would love him...I know they would. Your grandmother, too. She'd be proud of you."

"Everything ok?" Ethan asks.

Charity lets go of Rose and turns to hug Ethan. "More than ok."

"Little Cici, all grown up," Rose trails off cheerfully behind the counter. She hums and sways left and right as she finishes making the coffee.

Ethan taps his foot to the rhythm. Where has he heard that melody before? Not here...he would've remembered. Where? Charity watches him. It's no surprise to her that he can follow the count. But why does he seem like he knows

Love was in the Lost and Found

the song?

"Coffee and cookies, my little lovelies!" Rose sets everything on a tray.

Ethan and Charity both reach for the tray. She backs off. He picks up the tray and follows her. She walks to the table with the teddy bears.

"Charity, no one sits there," Ethan says. "Well...a long time ago there were these little girls that sat there but I haven't seen anyone sit there in years."

Charity takes the bears and put them in the basket. She sits in the chair and curls up. Ethan picks up the tray and walks robotically towards the table. Coffee splashes over the sides of the mugs. He watches her while taking cautious steps. She hugs her knees. He sets the tray down on the table and sits down. She grabs two cookies and hands him one. They break their cookies into halves. One half is put to the side. They look at each other. Cookie crumbles fall as they each break the half cookie in their hands. He hands her a quarter of a cookie; she hands one back in exchange.

"My parents used to sit over there..." she points at a table nearby. Tears form in her eyes. She puts the quarter bite of cookie into her mouth. "'Quarter size, perfect for one bite,' my mom used to say."

Ethan keeps his eyes on his cookie. "I'm sorry I kept forcing them on you..."

"My grandma said that these cookies are one of the first solid foods I've ever tried to eat," she takes another bite. She breaks the other half cookie into halves. She reaches over and feeds Ethan a quarter bite. He smiles and feeds her the

Love was in the Lost and Found

one that's still In hls hand. She turns away. "That one's all mushy. I want the other one."

He laughs and picks up the other one to feed her.

"You didn't force me to do anything," she accepts the cookie with a smile.

"When did you realize the little girl I was talking about is you?"

"I was curious when I saw you eating cookies, but you confirmed my theory when you told me."

"You had a theory about me?"

"Yup," she breaks the last half cookie and waves the small bite in front of Ethan's face. "You've been stalking me for years!"

He stops her hand in midair and holds onto her wrist. She looks at him. He eats the cookie in her hand. "So that means you were meant to be my wife."

Charity stands up and moves her chair next to Ethan's. She sits on his lap and rests her feet on the other chair. He turns to see if Rose is looking their way. Barely a glimpse of Rose can be seen.

"You're real...right?" Charity runs her fingers through Ethan's hair. "I'm not going to wake up one day and realize none of it existed."

"I keep asking the same about you..." he kisses her cheek. "Sometimes I wake up at night just to make sure I'm not sleeping on the sidewalk."

"But seriously though," she pokes his thigh repeatedly.

Love was in the Lost and Found

"Don't joke about marriage."

"Why do you always think I'm joking?"

She looks at her shoes and watch them sway left and right. He bought cookies and these shoes with his first paycheck. She lowers her feet to the floor and turns around to face him.

"The rest of our lives is a long time away..." Charity says.

"That's exactly why I should tie you down now. If another guy shows up, I'll be in deep..." Ethan says.

She forces a kiss on him before he can finish his sentence.

"Shut up. You had more girls than I had guys. I waited for you and you..."

"And I'm the last guy you'll ever need in your life."

"How many girls have you said that to?"

Ethan lays his head on Charity's shoulder. "How many guys have you wanted to marry?"

She grabs him by his ear. His cheeks turn bright red. "How many?"

Ethan hums the melody that Rose was humming. Charity loosens her grip.

"In a short short time, I met...," he tries to remember the lyrics as he sings.

"The love of my life," she corrects him. "How do you know this song?"

Love was in the Lost and Found 110

"If fate is playing jokes, I'm a willing victim," he keeps singing.

She puts her hand over his mouth. He continues humming. "How do you know this song?"

He stands to his feet and offers his hand. She looks up at him. "Tell me!" He offers his hand again. She takes it. He pulls her up and walks toward the door. She stops, "Where we going?"

"The park," he says. "You know the one."

Charity pulls him in the opposite direction. "Rose!" she screams. "I'm going to use the other door!"

Ethan looks around the coffee shop. Thank goodness it's empty. But, there aren't any other doors...

"Ok honey!" Rose's voice replies. "Make sure it closes all the way!"

Charity drags Ethan into what he always thought was a storage room. As it turns out, it is a storage room. There's just another door inside. She unlatches the top lock, unchains the second set, and twists the doorknob to open the door. It won't budge. He laughs.

"I almost forgot..." she mutters and runs her hand over the left side of the door. Her hand stops near the edge of the door. Crack. The door opens.

"Did you just..." he stares in shock.

"Come on," she walks outside. Once they both are standing outside she shuts the door and gives it a good kick. He crosses his arms and watches her. She pays no attention

Love was in the Lost and Found

to him and keeps walking. He catches up with her and holds her hand. The alley leads to one of the park's entrances. "Park. Now tell me, how do you know the song?"

Ethan points to the old swing set. Charity walks over and sits. He squats down next to her. "If this is a joke of fate..." he sings.

"Then we can start over again," Charity sings.

"The last time I saw you..." Ethan looks over by the monkey bars. "I stood over there."

He walks over and counts his steps. Seventeen steps. It used to be ten big steps. He turns and looks at Charity. She keeps her eyes on him. He takes ten big steps back to her. She locks her fingers in front her and plants her feet firmly on the ground. She closes her eyes as he moves closer to her.

"Destiny is written in your eyes," she sings. The warmth of his hand on her cheek frees the tears she had been holding back. She opens her eyes to see droplets leaving the corners of his eyes. She kisses him as their tears join forces and form a stream.

"I found my future the day you found me..." The two of them finish the song together.

Ethan sits down on the gravel and Charity slips off of the swing. She leans back against him and grabs his hands. Tears continue to fall as she hears her dad's voice, "Follow your heart, girlie girl..."

"That song's been stuck in my head for...I don't even know how many years." Ethan laughs.

"My dad wrote that song for my mom when he met her,"

Love was in the Lost and Found

Charity says. "They got married after two weeks."

"Two weeks! You mean I could've proposed to you the first night I crashed on your couch?" he brushes her hair to the side and lightly pecks her neck.

"You think I'd be crazy enough to say yes?"

"Well...you are the psychotic killer..."

Charity hums the melody and kisses the back of Ethan's hand. She sniffles and smiles as the tears keep rolling down. "You suck. You keep making me cry."

"It's ok to miss them...maybe we can keep their song as ours."

"No. You're writing me a new song."

"Say you'll marry me and it's a deal."

"It's a deal..."

"I wanna hear it."

"Ethan Winston, in sickness and in health, your wife, me, will be expecting you to write songs for me and me only."

Love was in the Lost and Found